Easy & Basic

餐飲口說 英語

林書平 ◎ 著

Upgrade餐飲服務口說英語
超強學習特色！

最Easy、好學的 口說英語

共**62組**簡短對話、每單元後附上**換句話說**、**重點句型**整理。
翻閱書頁時，書側的套色標籤設計可幫助即刻查找資訊，適合教學、自學！

最完整的 外場餐飲服務流程

從電話訂位‧接待、指引客人‧介紹菜單、點菜至結帳，
以及其他如外送、外帶餐點、各類餐點、客訴等**17大服務流程**

Bonus！4篇Advanced加碼

參加**異國美食展‧推廣生機、蔬食飲食篇**，
引領餐飲業在職人員靈活推廣美食
更進一步活用於各**餐飲流程**（如介紹菜單）中。

最擬真

模擬服務生接待3大客群（【**商務**】、【**家庭**】、【**導遊**】）的情境對話
模擬上菜、隨桌服務、準備會議、婚宴外燴時和顧客互動的方式，
提供英文表達上的小技巧，幫助餐飲從業人員於職場上更加得心應手！
提升顧客滿意度！

外師專業錄製MP3

作者序

　　很開心有這個機會，透過這本書，向各位分享我在義大利實習的所學經驗。當年遠赴歐洲義大利當地的飯店擔任實習助理，帶給了我許多文化衝擊及寶貴經驗，在經過實習時所遇到的經驗累積，讓我對於餐飲相關概念有了大致的了解。當時我負責的工作是飯店相關的翻譯，這個工作包含了需要去了解餐飲提供的服務項目，以及面對用餐的客人所提出的一些問題。本書於內容上，是我在歐洲實習所經歷過的相關經驗，由情境對話的方式，將可能遇到的狀況做一個簡單的呈現，唯恐學輕歷淺，若有疏誤之處，尚祈各方的不吝薔指教，非常感謝！

林書平

編者序

　　截至 2015 年年底為止，台灣中小企業依然以餐飲、服務業為大宗，民以食為天早已不言可喻，大街小巷做餐飲的店家已徹底融入民眾的日常生活裡。因此，不只是提供美食，如何為上門的顧客最好的服務，也是餐飲業主不斷求新求變的。邁向國際化即是提供良好服務的一種方式，台灣的餐飲業不能只顧及國內的需求，有時更有必要走出台灣，邁向世界，這時英語能力就非常重要了。

　　本書除了提供「必備」餐飲流程外，更加碼規劃、模擬餐飲業走出台灣的情境，讓餐飲英語不再侷限餐廳內，而是能活用於介紹美食，以及與各類顧客的應對上。每個大單元皆連接 3 個情境對話，每個情境對話都以關鍵句型緊扣大單元主題，再三加強句型的實用性，同時加深學習印象。換句話說、重要句型整理、職場小貼示，都是本書的特色。

編輯部

CONTENTS 目次

Easy & Basic 餐飲口說英語

Chapter 2　其他餐飲服務英語會話 Conversational English for Other Dining Services

Unit
01　訂位
Reservation

1.1 情境對話──和商務客的應答
Dialogue with Business Customers

 Track 01

*Waiter 服務生，簡稱 **W**。*

*Guest, Mr. Brown 商務客，Brown 先生，簡稱 **G**。*

The restaurant telephone is ringing now.

W: Good evening, Michael's **Steak** House. How may I help you?

G: Hello. I'd like to reserve a table for Thursday evening, please.

W: Certainly. And for how many people, sir?

G: Ten people actually. By the way, it's for business **purpose**. Could we reserve a private room?

W: Certainly, sir. At what time on Thursday evening?

G: About 6:30 PM.

W: Ok, I'll book a private room for ten people for you. Could you please give me your name and phone number, sir?

G: Steve Brown. My phone number is 3899-0099.

W: Ok, Mr. Brown. The reservation is **completed**.

G: By the way, we are here to attend the exhibition. Will there be any space in the private room for us to use the projector?

W: No problem, sir. Anything else? We offer a discount for guests who come here for the exhibition.

G: Thank you for asking. Please also prepare a **case** of champagne.

W: Ok, sir.

Unit 01

中文翻譯

餐廳電話正響起……

W：晚安您好，這裡是麥可牛排館。請問有我可以效勞的地方嗎？

G：你好。我想要預訂禮拜四晚上的位子。

W：好的。請問要訂幾位呢，先生？

G：我們會有十位，這是商務聚餐。我們可以訂包廂嗎？

W：當然可以，先生。要訂禮拜四晚上幾點呢？

G：大約晚上六點半。

W：好的，我將為您預定一間包廂，十位客人。可以麻煩給我您的姓名及電話號碼嗎，先生？

G：Steve Brown。我的電話號碼是 3899-0099。

W：好的，Brown 先生。您的訂位已經完成。

G：對了，我們是來此是為了參加展覽，請問包廂內有空間可以讓我們使用投影機嗎？

W：沒問題，先生。還有別的需要嗎？我們有給來此參展的顧客折扣。

G：謝謝您特地詢問，那麼請幫我準備一箱的香檳。

W：好的，先生。

單字 Vocabulary

1. **steak** *n.* 牛排、肉排

   例 There is a very tasty steak house in the downtown; you should go to try it.
   在城內有一間很好吃的牛排館，你應該去試試看。

2. **purpose** *n.* 意圖、目的、用途

   例 I don't know the purpose of his visit.
   我不知道他來的目的為何。

3. **complete** *v.* 完成

   例 I have completed all the courses I need for the freshmen year. homework.
   我已經完成所有大一生必修的課程家庭作業了。

4. **case** *n.* 箱、盒、容器

   例 The equipment is stored in a huge case.
   此設備收納於大箱子中。

1.2 情境對話——和家庭客的應答
Dialogue with Family Guests

 Track 02

 Waiter 服務生，簡稱 W。

 Guest, Mr. Brown 家庭客，Brown 先生，簡稱 G。

The restaurant telephone is ringing now...

W: Good evening, this is Happy Friday Restaurant. How may I help you?

G: Good evening. I'd like to book a table for Saturday noon.

W: Certainly, sir. What time would you like your table?

G: About 12:30 PM.

W: I'm afraid that there is no available table at this time. Would you like to change the reservation time?

G: How about 1:00 PM?

W: I'll check for it. Please hold on a second.

G: Sure.

W: Sir, we still have one available table for you at 1:00 PM.

G: Good.

W: How many people will there be in your party?

G: Four adults and two children.

W: Since you have children, are there any special request we can provide in advance?

G: Yes, two child seats, please. And we can't have spicy foods. Please help us to avoid that.

W: No problem, sir. Could you please give me your name and phone number?

G: Jordon Brown. 5644-8900.

W: Ok, Mr. Brown. Your booking is confirmed. Thanks for calling. We look forward to seeing you this Saturday noon.

中文翻譯

餐廳電話正響起……

W：晚安您好，這裡是快樂星期五餐廳。請問有我可以效勞的地方嗎？

G：晚安。我想要預訂禮拜六中午的位子。

W：好的，先生。請問您要訂幾點的呢？

G：大約中午十二點半。

W：這個時段恐怕是沒有位子了。您想要訂早一點的或是晚一點的位子嗎？

G：那下午一點呢？

W：我查一下。請您稍等一下。

G：沒問題。

W：先生，下午一點還有位子。

G：很好。

W：請問您要訂幾位呢？

G：四個大人，兩個小孩。

W：由於您有帶小朋友，所以有需要我們餐廳事先幫您準備什麼嗎？

G：好的，請準備兩張兒童椅。還有，我們沒辦法吃辣，請幫我們避開。

W：沒問題，先生。請您給我您的姓名與電話號碼。

G：Jordon Brown，5644-8900。

W：好的，Brown 先生。您已確定訂位。感謝您的來電，我們期待禮拜六中午與您相見。

單字 Vocabulary

1. **request** *n.* 要求、請求
   例 Can I ask for another request in designing the ring for my girlfriend?
   我可以額外要求設計在那個要送我女朋友的戒指上嗎？

2. **spicy** *adj.* 辣的
   例 The restaurant is known for its spicy food.
   這間餐廳的菜辣得非常有名。

3. **avoid** *v.* 避免
   例 To stay healthy, we should avoid having heavy meals too often.
   為了保持健康，我們應該避免太常餐餐大魚大肉。

1.3 情境對話——和團體客導遊的應答
Dialogue with Tour Guides

Track 03

Waiter，簡稱 W。

Tour Guide, Ms. Brown 導遊，Brown 小姐，簡稱 T。

The restaurant telephone is ringing now...

W: Good evening, this is Milano Italian Restaurant. How may I help you?

T: Hello. I'd like to make a reservation.

W: **(the waiter can't hear Miss Brown on the phone clearly)** I **beg** your **pardon**?

T: I'd like to make a reservation on May 15 evening.

W: Certainly, madam. At what time on May 15 evening?

T: About 6:30 PM.

W: For how many people?

T: For 16 people. It's a tour group from Taiwan. I'd like to book a private room for them. Is there any private room available?

W: Yes, madam. Could you give me your name and number?

T: Judy Brown. The phone number is 4566-0988.

W: Ok, Miss Brown. May I confirm the booking with you again?

T: Sure.

W: You have booked one private room for 16 people on May 15 evening 6:30 PM. Is that correct?

T: That's right.

W: Ok, madam. The booking is in the process. Any special request for foods?

T: Thank you for reminding me. Most tourists in this group are the elderly, so we prefer to have light foods. Thank you.

W: We will take care of that, madam. And the reservation is well completed. Thanks for calling. We look forward to having you with us on May 15 evening. Good bye.

Unit 01

中文翻譯

餐廳電話正響起……

W：晚安您好，這裡米蘭義式餐館。請問有我可以效勞的地方嗎？

T：哈囉，我想要預訂位子。

W：（餐廳服務生沒有聽清楚 Brown 小姐說的）不好意思，請您再說一次？

T：我想要預訂五月十五號晚上的位子。

W：好的，女士。五月十五號晚上幾點呢？

T：大約晚上六點半。

W：請問幾位呢？

T：十六位，這是個從台灣來的旅行團。我想要為他們訂個包廂，請問還有空的包廂嗎？

W：有的，女士。請您給我您的姓名與電話。

T：Judy Brown，我的電話號碼是 4566-0988。

W：好的，Brown 小姐。我可以再與您確認一次訂位資料嗎？

T：當然可以。

W：五月十五日晚上六點半，一間包廂，十六位客人。這樣正確嗎？

T：這樣沒錯。

W：好的，女士。還在處理中，請問食物上有任何需求嗎？

T：謝謝您提醒我。我們這團的旅客大多是老年人，所以我們希望食物清淡點。謝謝。

W：我們會注意的。訂位也已完成。感謝您的來電，我們期待五月十五號晚上與您見面，再見！

Unit 01

單字 Vocabulary

1. **beg** *n.* （禮貌用語）請（允許）……；請（原諒）……
   例 I beg the suggestion of the new annual operating plan.
   我請求允許年度新營運計劃的建議。

2. **pardon** *n.* 原諒、寬恕
   例 I beg your pardon. I should confirm the available time before visiting you.
   請原諒我冒昧。我應該在拜訪您前先確認您可以的時間。

1.4 換句話說 In Other Words

I'm afraid that there is no available table at this time.

這時間恐怕是沒有空的位子了。

🍵 **I'm afraid we are fully booked for this time.**

這時間恐怕是沒有空的位子了。

🍵 **There is no vacant table at this time.**

這個時間沒有空桌。

🍵 **I'm afraid that there is no table available for the time you requested.**

您要求這個時間恐怕沒有空的位子。

What time would you like your table?

您想訂幾點的位子呢？

🍵 **What time do you want to have the table?**

您想訂幾點的位子呢？

🍵 **At what time do you want to book?**

您想訂幾點的位子呢？

🍵 **What time do you want to reserve?**

您想訂幾點的位子呢？

Ten people, actually. By the way it's for business purpose.
我們會有十位，這是商務聚餐。

There will be ten people to attend the business meal.
將會有十位人士來三家商業聚餐。

I would like to order a table for ten people.
我想要預訂十個人的位子。

It's a party of ten people, and we want to reserve the business meal set.
我們有十人要吃商業聚餐。

Since you have children, are there any special request that we can provide in advance?
由於您有帶小朋友，所以有需要我們餐廳事先幫您準備什麼嗎？

Anything that I can prepare for your children in advance?
有什麼可以事先為您的小朋友做準備的嗎？

Would you like some early preparations for your children?
您想要替您的小朋友提早準備些什麼嗎。

We provide the preorder for children. Would you like to have this service?
我們為小朋友提供預訂服務。您想要使用這項服務嗎？

Unit 02 確認及取消訂位 Booking Confirmation and Cancellation

情境對話——和商務客的應答
Dialogue with Business Customers

 Track 04

Waiter 服務生，簡稱 W。

Guest, Mr. Brown 商務客，Brown 先生，簡稱 G。

The restaurant telephone is ringing now.

W: Good evening, Michael's Steak House. How may I help you?

G: Hello. I'd like to confirm with you to see if my reservation is completed.

W: No problem, sir. Could you please give me the booking **information**? Your name and phone number, please?

G: Steve Brown and the phone number is 3899-0099.

W: Hold on a second, please.

G: Sure.

W: Mr. Brown, you have reserved one private room for ten people on Thursday evening at 6:30 PM. Is that correct?

G: Yes, it's correct. By the way, I'd like to know if there is a parking space for guests.

W: I'm afraid that we don't provide the parking lot for our guests. It's hard to find a spare space to be the parking lot in the downtown. I suggest that you take the metro or other public transportation.

G: I see. Thanks a lot.

W: You're welcome, sir. Is there anything I can do for you?

G: Our guests are not familiar with the area around your restaurant. Where can we get the transportation guide?

W: You can go to our website and check the icon titled "Transportation". There is detailed information about how to get here. If you still have a problem with that, please don't hesitate to call us.

G: Thank you. You helped a lot.

Unit 02

中文翻譯

餐廳電話正響起……

W：晚安您好，這裡是麥可牛排館。請問有我可以效勞的地方嗎？

G：你好，我想要確認一下我的訂位。

W：沒問題，先生。可以麻煩您給我您的訂位資料嗎？您的姓名及電話號碼是？

G：Steve Brown，電話號碼是 3899-0099。

W：請您稍等。

G：好的。

W：Brown 先生，您是預定星期四晚上六點半，十人的包廂，這樣對嗎？

G：是的，正確。對了，我想知道您們是否有提供客人的停車場。

W：很抱歉，我們沒有提供客人停車場的服務。在市區內不是那麼容易找到多餘的地方做為停車場。我建議您可以搭乘捷運或是其他大眾運輸工具。

G：我瞭解了，非常謝謝。

W：您別客氣，先生。還有我能協助的地方嗎？

G：我們對於餐廳周圍不太熟悉，要去哪取得交通資訊呢？

W：您可至我們的官網，點選「交通方式」的按鈕，裡面就有來此詳細的資訊了。若您還有問題，也請來電詢問。

G：謝謝您幫了很多。

單字 Vocabulary

1. **information** *n.* 資料
   例 We need the information as detailed as possible.
   我要這份資料月詳細越好。

2. **spare** *adj.* 多餘的
   例 We need a spare space in the warehouse to store inventory.
   倉庫需要一個空間擺放庫存。

3. **icon** *n.* 標籤；指標性的（人、事、物）
   例1 Click the icon and you will get what you want there.
   點進標籤進去後，你就能找到你想要的。
   例2 They are the icon of the pop music in the 90s.
   他們是 90 年代流行音樂的指標。

4. **Sb have a problem with** *ph.* 有問題
   例 If you still have a problem with that, please tell us.
   若您對此還有問題，請告訴我們。

2.2 情境對話──和家庭客的應答
Dialogue with Family Guests

 Track 05

 Waiter 服務生，簡稱 W。

 *Guest, Mr. Brown 家庭客，Brown 先生，簡稱 **G**。*

The restaurant telephone is ringing now.

W: Good evening, this is Happy Friday Restaurant. How may I help you?

G: Hello. Yes, I'd like to cancel my reservation.

W: No problem, sir. Could you please give me the booking information? Your name and phone number, please?

G: Jordon Brown. 5644-8900.

W: Please wait a second for the cancellation.

G: Ok.

W: **(one minute later...)** Sir, we can't find your booking information from our system, yet. May I ask for your name and phone number once again?

G: It's Jordon Brown. 5644-8900.

W: Thank you. Right. I **misspelled** your name. Sorry, sir. The process is going now.

(one minute later...)

W: Sir, the cancellation is completed. Thank you for your patience. Is there anything I can help?

G: No, It's Ok. I'm really sorry for the inconvenience.

W: No problem, sir. We look forward to having you with us soon. Have a nice day!

中文翻譯

餐廳電話正響起⋯⋯

W：晚安您好，這裡是快樂星期五餐廳。請問有我可以效勞的地方嗎？

G：你好。是的，我想要取消訂位。

W：沒問題的，先生。可以麻煩您給我您的訂位資料嗎？您的姓名及電話號碼是？

G：Jordon Brown. 5644-8900.

W：請稍等，取消作業正在進行。

G：好的。

W：（一分鐘後⋯⋯）先生，我們的系統找不到您的訂位資料。可以再請您提供一次姓名和電話號碼嗎？

G：Jordon Brown. 5644-8900.

W：謝謝您。很抱歉我拼錯您的名字了。正在取消訂位了。

（一分鐘後……）

W：先生，您的訂位已經完成取消。感謝您的耐心，還有我能幫助的地方嗎？

G：不用了，沒關係。造成您的不便，我很抱歉。

W：沒關係的，先生。我們期待下次與您見面，祝您有美好的一天！

G：造成您的不便，我很抱歉。

W：沒關係的，先生。我們期待下次與您見面，祝您有美好的一天！

單字 Vocabulary

1. **misspell** *v.* 拼錯
   例 The student has misspelled his name.
   這位學生拼錯了他的名字。

2. **cancellation** *n.* 取消
   例 The system is processing the cancellation.
   系統正在處理取消流程。

2.3 情境對話──和團體客導遊的應答
Dialogue with Tour Guides

🔘 *Track 06*

Waiter，簡稱 W。

Tour Guide, Ms. Brown 導遊，Brown 小姐，簡稱 T。

The restaurant telephone is ringing now.

W: Good evening, this is Milano Italian Restaurant. How may I help you?

T: Good evening. I'd like to double check the reservation.

W: Yes, madam. Could you please give me your name and the phone number for the confirmation?

T: Judy Brown. The phone number is 4566-0988

W: Please hold on a second, madam. **(one minute later...)** Madam, you have reserved a private room for 16 people on May 15 evening at 6:30 PM. Is that correct?

T: Yes, it's correct. Because it is a tour group from Taiwan, I do hope that they will have an **unforgettable** memory after tasting the Italian cuisine. And, I'm wondering if it is possible for the restaurant to provide the specialties for those visitors.

W: I don't think that would be a problem.

T: That's great! Especially for desserts.

W: That's no problem, madam. Our restaurant is famous for genuine Tiramisu and cheese cake. We'll try to make a little different from traditional ones. Do you have any special requests for food?

T: Thanks for asking. We have three vegetarian members and one having an egg allergy. Is it ok for you to prepare foods that meet their needs in advance?

W: You're welcome, madam. That's no problem. If there is any other requests, please just feel free to contact us. Have a nice day!

Unit 02

中文翻譯

餐廳電話正響起⋯⋯

W：晚安您好，這裡是米蘭義式餐館。請問有我可以效勞的地方嗎？

T：晚安。我想要再確認一下訂位。

W：好的，女士。可以麻煩您給我您提供訂位的姓名及電話號碼，讓我做確認嗎？

T：Judy Brown，電話號碼是 4566-0988。

W：請您稍等，女士。（一分鐘後⋯⋯）女士，您預定五月十五日晚上六點半，一間包廂，十六人。這樣正確嗎？

T：是的，正確無誤。因為這是一個來自台灣的旅遊團，我希望他們嚐過這裡的義式美食後，可以有個難忘的回憶。我在想，你們餐廳是否有可能提供特別的餐點給他們呢？

W：關於準備特別餐點給外國旅客是沒有問題的。

T：太棒了。特別是甜點喔。

W：沒問題，女士。我們餐廳最有名的就道地的提拉米蘇及芝士蛋糕。我們會試著在傳統的甜點上做點小變化。請問您們在食物上有任何要求嗎？

T：非常謝謝。謝謝您特地詢問。我們有三個團員吃素，一個對蛋有過敏，請問您能事先準備好他們的食物嗎。

W：您別客氣，女士，沒有問題，如果您還有其他需求，請您別客氣與
　我們聯繫。祝您有個美好的一天！

單字 Vocabulary

1. **unforgettable** *adj.* 難忘的
   例 People have different definitions about an unforgettable memory.
   人們對一個難忘的回憶有不同的定義。

2. **specialty** *n.* 特餐、名菜
   例 You can taste a wide variety of local specialties in this restaurant.
   您可在這間餐廳品嚐到多種當地名菜。

3. **genuine** *adj.* 名副其實的、道地的
   例 The sweet shop serves genuine Tiramisu.
   這間甜點店販賣道地的提拉米蘇。

4. **allergy** *n.* 過敏
   例 The medicine is prescribed to treat the allergy.
   這藥是開來治過敏的。

2.4 換句話說 In Other Words

I'd like to confirm with you to see if my reservation is completed.

我想要確認一下我的訂位。

🍵 **I want to check my booking again.**

我想要確認一下我的訂位。

🍵 **I would like to see if my booking is well completed.**

我想要確認一下我的訂位。

🍵 **I would like to double check my reservation.**

我想要確認一下我的訂位。

Could you please give me your name and the phone number for the confirmation?

可以麻煩您給我您提供訂位的姓名及電話號碼，讓我做確認嗎？

🍵 **Sir, I would like to have your name and number to check your reservation.**

先生，我想要您的姓名及電話來確認訂位。

🍵 **Would you please kindly provide the booking name and phone number for reconfirmation?**

您可以麻煩提供訂位姓名及電話號碼來確認訂位嗎？

🍵 **May I have your name and number for checking your reservation?**

請問我可以問一下您的姓名及電話來確認訂位嗎？

Hold on a second please.

請您稍等。

Please wait a second.
請稍候。

Please give me a second.
請給我一些時間。

Please kindly wait for a moment.
請稍等片刻。

I'd like to know if there is a parking space for guests.

我想知道您們是否有提供客人的停車場。

Is there any free parking space?
有免費的停車場嗎？

Do you provide the parking space for free?
你們有提供免費停車嗎？

I would like to know where I can park my car for free?
我想知道哪邊可以免費停車的？

Unit
03

接待及指引客人
Ushering Guests into Their Seats

3.1 情境對話——和商務客的應答
Dialogue with Business Customers

 Track 07

*Waiter 服務生，簡稱 **W**。*

*Guest, Mr. Brown 商務客，Brown 先生，簡稱 **G**。*

W: Good evening, welcome to Happy Friday Restaurant. May I help you?

G: Yes, we have a reservation at 6:30 PM under Jason Brown.

W: Let me take a look. A private room for ten?

G: Yes.

W: The **private** room is ready. This way, please.

G: We are still waiting for the other two **vendors**. They are not here yet.

W: I see. Would you like to be **seated** while waiting?

G: Thank you.

W: Here is the menu for you while waiting. If you need some water, please let us know.

G: OK.

Ten minutes later...

G: The other two vendors just called and told me they will be late, so we would like to start the meal first.

W: I see, sir. I'll usher the other two guests to the private room when they **arrive**.

G: Thank you.

W: Please mind your step and kindly notice that the private room is a non-smoking area.

G: I see.

Unit 03

中文翻譯

W：晚安您好，這裡是快樂星期五餐廳。請問有我可以效勞的地方嗎？

G：是的，我們預定晚上六點半的訂位，訂位人是 Jason Brown。

W：讓我查一下。是十人，一間包廂嗎？

G：是的。

W：包廂已經準備好了，這邊請。

G：我們還在等其他兩位廠商，他們還沒有到。

W：我瞭解了。那您要坐著等他們來嗎？

G：謝謝。

W：先生這是菜單，您可以先看看。若您需要開水，也可跟我們說。

G：好的。

十分鐘後……

G：另外兩位廠商剛剛打電話來告訴我，他們會晚點到，所以我們想先開始用餐。

W：我瞭解了。待他們兩位抵達後，我將會帶領他們兩位進包廂。

G：謝謝你。

W：請小心台階。提醒您，包廂內是禁止抽菸的。

G：我知道了。

單字 Vocabulary

1. **private** *adj.* 私人的、個人的
   例1 That is my private opinion.
   這是我個人的意見。
   例2 We all need private space when we are alone.
   每個人獨處時都需要一些私人的空間。

2. **vendor** *n.* 廠商
   例 The company asked for some discounts from the vendor.
   公司向廠商要了一些折扣。

3. **seated** *adj.* 就座
   例 Please be seated here and wait for a while.
   請在這裡就座，並稍待一會。

4. **arrive** *v.* 抵達、到達
   例 The train will arrive at Taipei at 6 PM.
   火車將會於晚間六點抵達台北。

3.2 情境對話──和家庭客的應答
Dialogue with Family Guests

 Track 08

 *Waiter 服務生，簡稱 **W**。*

 *Guest, Mr. Brown 家庭客，Brown 先生，簡稱 **G**。*

W: Good evening, this is Happy Friday Restaurant. May I help you?

G: Yes. We would like to have a table for three.

W: Have you made the reservation?

G: No.

W: Ok, we still need to check if there are still available tables for you. It will take a while since it's a bit packed today.

Two minutes later...

W: Sir, we still have tables available for three. Would you come with me, please?

G: Yes, thank you. Is that a non-smoking area? My mother is **allergic** to the smell of cigarette. Sorry for the inconvenience.

W: Sir. There are no available tables in the non-smoking area for now. I'm afraid you would need to wait for a while.

G: How long are we going to wait?

W: About 10-20 minutes. Is that ok with you?

G: Ok. We will wait.

W: **(One minute later...)** Sir, we got a table reservation in the non-smoking area cancelled. The table is available now. This way, please.

G: Great!

W: Ok. **Mind** your head here.

G: Thank you.

W: Where would you **prefer** to sit?

G: I would like to sit by the window.

W: **(Pulling the chair for the man...)** Is this seat ok?

G: It's good. Thank you.

W: You're welcome, sir. Here are the menus for you. And I'll be back later, ok?

G: Sure.

Unit 03

中文翻譯

W：晚安您好，這裡是快樂星期五餐廳。請問有我可以效勞的地方嗎？

G：是的，我們想要一張三人的座位。

W：請問您有訂位嗎？

G：沒有。

W：好的，那麼我們還要確認一下現在有沒有位置。今天人有點多，可能要花一點時間喔。

（兩分鐘後……）

W：先生，我們還有一桌三個人的位置，可以請您跟我來嗎？

G：好的，謝謝您。請問那是非吸煙區嗎？我母親對香菸的味道過敏。很抱歉帶來不便。

W：先生，現在非吸菸區沒有位置了，我想您可能還要再等一等。

G：要等多久呢？

W：大概 10 ～ 20 分鐘，這樣您可以嗎？

G：好的，可以。

（一分鐘後……）

W：先生，非吸菸區有一桌位置訂位取消了，您可以來用了，這邊請。

G：太好了。

W：好的。這裡請您小心，別撞著頭了。

G：謝謝。

W：您想要坐哪邊呢？

G：我想要靠窗的位子。

W：（**為男士拉椅子⋯⋯**）這裡可以嗎？

G：這裡很好，謝謝。

W：您別客氣，先生。這是給您參考的菜單，我稍會兒在過來，好嗎？

G：當然可以。

單字 Vocabulary

1. **allergic** *adj.* 過敏的
   例 Tina is allergic to seafood.
   Tina 對海鮮過敏。

2. **mind** *v.* 注意、留意
   例 Please mind the gap while moving.
   在移動時請留意台階。

3. **prefer** *v.* 更喜歡、寧願
   例 I prefer staying at home to going out with him.
   比起跟他一起出門，我更喜歡待在家裡。

3.3 情境對話——和團體客導遊的應答
Dialogue with Tour Guides

Track 09

Waiter，簡稱 W。

Tour Guide, Ms. Brown 導遊，Brown 小姐，簡稱 T。

W: Good evening, welcome to Milano Italian Restaurant. May I help you?

T: Yes, we made a reservation this evening at 6:30 PM under Judy Brown. It's a 16 person group.

W: Ok, let me take a look. **(one minute later...)** Yes, Miss Brown. Have all the guests arrived here?

T: Not yet. We are still waiting for the other five guests. They are on the way now. But I think we could take a rest in the private room first and wait for the rest to come.

W: Ok. The private room is ready now. This way, please.

T: Thank you.

W: You are welcome, madam. We will usher the others when they arrive.

T: That will be great.

The group members who arrived early are following the waiter.

W: This way, please. Please mind your step here.

T: Ok.

W: Here is the private room for you. There are two restrooms on the second floor and the third floor respectively. You can go this way, turn left at the end of hall and go upstairs. You will see the restrooms right up there.

T: Thank you.

W: Here are the menus and I'll be back to take the order.

T: Ok.

Unit 03

中文翻譯

W：晚安您好，這裡是米蘭義式餐館。請問有我可以效勞的地方嗎？

T：是的，我們有訂今晚六點半的位置，是個十六人的團體。

W：好的，讓我查一下。（一分鐘後⋯⋯）是的，Brown 小姐。請問客人都已經到了嗎？

T：還沒。我們還在等其他五位客人，他們在路上了。但我想我們可以先到包廂休息，等其他人來。

W：好的，包廂已經準備好了。您要坐下來稍等一下嗎？

T：謝謝你。

W：您別客氣，女士。等其他人到後，我們會帶他們到這裡。

T：這樣就太好了。

先抵達的團員跟著服務生⋯⋯

W：這邊請。請小心步伐。

T：好的。

W：這是您預定的包廂。這裡有兩間洗手間，分別在二樓及三樓。您可以走這邊，大廳走到底左轉上樓後，您會看到洗手間了。

T：謝謝你。

W：這是菜單，我稍會再回來為您點餐。

T：好的。

單字 Vocabulary

1. **respectively** *adv.* 分別地
   例 The workers and the salesclerks got 4% and 3% pay rises respectively.
   工人及銷售員分別加薪 4% 及 3%。

2. **turn** *v.* 轉彎、轉向
   例 Go straight and turn right. You'll see the supermarket is right there.
   直走後右轉，你會看到超市就在那裡。

3. **upstairs** *adv.* 往樓上、在樓上
   例 She went upstairs directly to her room.
   她直接上樓到她的房間。

4. **restroom** *n.* 廁所（美式用法，英式用法為 toilet。）
   例 The restroom is on your right side.
   廁所在您的右手邊。

Unit 03

3.4 換句話說 In Other Words

This way, please.

這邊請。

 Would you come with me, please?
請跟我來。

Please come with me this way.
請跟我這邊走。

Would you please follow me?
請跟我來，好嗎？

Where would you prefer to sit?

您想要坐哪裡呢？

Where would you like to sit?
您想要坐哪裡呢？

Where would you like for your table?
您想要坐哪裡呢？

Where would you like to be seated?
您想要坐哪裡呢？

Would you like to be seated while waiting?

那您要坐著等他們來嗎？

- **Would you like to wait for them here?**
  您想在這邊稍後嗎？
- **Would you like to go first or wait until they come?**
  您想要先進去，還是等他們來呢？
- **You may have a seat here while waiting.**
  您可以坐在這邊等候。

The other two vendors just called and told me that they will be late, so we would like to start the meal first.

另外兩位廠商剛剛打電話來告訴我，他們會晚點到，所以我們想先開始用餐。

- **I just got the phone call and be informed that they will be late, so we would like to start the dinner first.**
  我剛接到電話，他們會晚點到，所以我們想先開始用餐。
- **They just phoned me and informed that they will be late for a while, so we want to start the dinner first.**
  他們剛才打給我，告訴我會晚點到，所以我們想先開始用晚餐。
- **I think it's better to start the meal because my two vendors are being late.**
  我覺得先開始用餐比較好，因為我的兩位廠商會晚一點到。

Unit 03

47

Unit
04

介紹菜單及點菜
Introducing Dishes and Taking an Order

4.1 情境對話——和商務客的應答
Dialogue with Business Customers

Track 10

Waiter 服務生，簡稱 W。

Guest, Mr. Brown 商務客，Brown 先生，簡稱 G。

W: Hello, my name is Emily. I'll be your server this evening. May I take your order now?

G: Not yet. We need to take a look for a little while, or you can introduce the dishes for us? Thank you.

W: No problem, sir. Our special for this evening is a Fresh Crispy Calamari and Original Baby Back Ribs. The Fresh Crispy Calamari is famous for its special sauce that tastes slightly spicy. The Original Baby Back Ribs are richly seasoned with selected spices and slowly smoked to mouthwatering perfection. You can select one of our four signature sauces written at the bottom of the menu on page three.

G: Ok, we are ready to take an order now.

W: Ok, sir. What would you like to order?

G: Original Baby Back Ribs with original sauce.

W: A very good choice. Would you like soup or salad with that?

G: I'll have an onion soup, please.

W: Ok. And how about the other three guests?

G: We will have the same, please.

W: Certainly, sir. Anything to drink?

G: We would like to have three cups of coffee. And one bottle of sparkling water. Also, we'd like to have our drinks served first.

W: No problem, sir. I'll be back with a bottle of sparkling water and other drinks for you shortly. Anything else I can help you with?

G: No, thank you.

Unit 04

中文翻譯

W：哈囉，我是 Emily，今晚由我為您服務。請問您要點餐了嗎？

G：還沒，我們需要一點時間再看一下菜單，還是你可以幫我們介紹餐點嗎？謝謝您。

W：沒問題的，先生。我們今晚的特餐為香酥章魚及經典嫩烤豬肋排。本餐廳的香酥章魚，以搭配微微辣味的特殊佐醬聞名。經典嫩烤豬肋排經過嚴選香料佐味及慢火碳烤，呈現出讓您口水直流的樣貌，您可以搭配其中一種我們的招牌醬料，在第三頁菜單的下方。

G：好的，我們已經可以點餐了。

W：好的，先生。請問要點什麼呢？

G：經典嫩烤豬肋排，搭配經典原味佐料。

W：非常棒的選擇。您要搭配湯品或沙拉嗎？

G：來一份洋蔥湯，謝謝。

W：好的。其他三位貴賓要點什麼呢？

G：我們要一樣的餐點，謝謝。

W：沒問題的，先生。要喝點什麼嗎？

G：請給我們三杯咖啡，一瓶氣泡水。我們的飲料要先上。

W：沒問題，先生。我稍後將氣泡水和飲料送過來給您。還有我能協助的地方嗎？

G：沒有了，謝謝。

單字 Vocabulary

1. **crispy** *adj.* 脆脆的
   例 I want some crispy toppings on the ice cream.
   我想在冰淇淋上加一些脆脆的配料。

2. **season** *v.* 給……調味
   例 Mom seasoned the fish with some sugar and vinegar.
   媽媽用一些糖與醋來給魚調味。

3. **mouthwatering** *adj.* 令人垂涎的
   例 The delicious dishes make me mouthwatering.
   這道美味的料理讓我垂涎三尺。

4. **signature** *n.* 特色
   例 This is our signature dish. Please do try this.
   這是我們的特色料理，請務必試一試。

5. **sauce** *n.* 醬汁、佐醬
   例 The orange sauce matched the dish very well.
   桔子醬汁與這倒菜真的很對味。

情境對話——和家庭客的應答
Dialogue with Family Guests

 Track 11

 Waiter 服務生，簡稱 W。

 Guest, Mr. Brown 家庭客，Brown 先生，簡稱 G。

W: Hello, my name is Hanna. I'll be your **server** this evening. May I take your order now?

G: Not yet. Every dish looks tasty. Could we have some time?

W: Sure. I'll be back later. Just take your time.

Five minutes later...

W: Well, have you **decided** what you like to have tonight?

G: Yes, we are ready to **order** now.

W: What would you like to order, sir?

G: I would like to have Red Hot Buffalo Wings and a Mozzarella Cheese for appetizer. A Caesar Salad, a Baked Potato Soup and two New York Steaks.

W: How would you like your steaks?

G: Both medium rare, please.

W: Anything else, sir?

G: Any kids meal provided?

W: Yes, sir. Please turn to page five, the kids menu is shown on the bottom of the page. We have provided Cheeseburgers and Chicken Pasta with cream for kids.

G: Then I'll have one Cheeseburger without pepper for my kid.

W: One Cheeseburger without pepper. How about drinks?

G: Right, two cups of Cappuccino for adults; one glass of orange juice for the kid.

W: Sure. We will send the meal soon.

Unit 04

中文翻譯

W：哈囉，我是 Hanna，今晚由我為您服務。請問您要點餐了嗎？

G：還沒，每道菜都很美味的樣子。我們可以再多一點時間看菜單嗎？

W：當然可以，我稍會兒再過來，您慢慢看。

五分鐘過後……

W：請問決定好今晚要吃些什麼了嗎？

G：是的，我們可以點餐了。

W：您想要點什麼餐點呢，先生？

G：我想要一份水牛城香辣雞翅及摩札瑞拉起司作為開胃菜。一份凱薩沙
　　拉、烤馬鈴薯濃湯及兩份牛排。

W：您想要牛排幾分熟呢？

G：都五分熟，謝謝。

W：還有別的需要嗎？

G：有提供兒童餐嗎？

W：有的，先生。請翻到菜單第五頁，兒童餐在菜單下方。我們有提供
　　起司漢堡及雞肉奶油義大利麵。

G：那我要點一個起司漢堡。不要胡椒粉。

W：一個起司漢堡不要胡椒粉。想喝什麼飲料嗎？

G：有，兩杯卡布其諾給大人；小孩要一杯橘子果汁。

W：好的，等下餐點就會送上來。

單字 Vocabulary

1. **server** *n.* 侍者
   例 To be a server, the attitude is very important.
   身為一名侍者，接待客戶的態度非常重要。

2. **decide** *v.* 決定
   例 It's hard to decide where to take a vacation during the New Year holidays.
   很難決定在新年假期要去哪裡度假。

3. **order** *v.* 點餐
   例 I would like to order a cup of coffee, please.
   我想要點一杯咖啡，麻煩你。

4.3 情境對話——和團體客導遊的應答
Dialogue with Tour Guides

Track 12

Waiter，簡稱 *W*。

Tour Guide, Ms. Brown 導遊，*Brown* 小姐，簡稱 *T*。

W: Hello, my name is Hank. I'll be your server this evening. Here is the menu for your guests.

T: That's great. Could you briefly **introduce** what you have on the menu for us?

W: That's no problem, madam. Our special for today is Live Lobster & Rib Combo and South Miami Fried Shrimp. Chicken Caesar Flatbread for appetizer. Milano's Dinner Salad, French Onion Soup and Signature Tiramisu. We also have vegetarian sets if you need.

T: Sounds **delicious**!

W: Would you like to order now?

T: Not yet. I have to **discuss** the menu with my group members. I'll let you know when we are ready to order.

W: No problem, madam. Would you like to have something to drink before ordering?

T: That might be good. I think my group members are thirsty now. Please bring us some water and lemonade.

W: No problem, madam. I'll bring the beverage to the guests shortly.

T: Thank you so much.

W: You are welcome, madam. If you have anything else I can help you with, please let us know.

T: Yes, I found some of my group members don't have forks or napkins. Would you please bring some for us now?

W: Sorry, madam. We send them for you immediately.

Unit 04

中文翻譯

W：哈囉，我是 Hanna，今晚由我為您服務。這是提供您的特餐菜單。

T：太棒了。請你為我們簡單介紹一下菜單，好嗎？

W：沒問題，女士。本餐廳今日特餐是新鮮龍蝦與肋排組合餐及邁阿密炸蝦，開胃菜為雞肉凱薩薄餅，還有招牌沙拉、法式洋蔥濃湯及招牌提拉米蘇。如果有需要，我們也有蔬食餐喔。

T：好像很美味的樣子。

W：請問您要點餐了嗎？

T：還沒，我必須與我的團員討論一下菜單。我稍會兒會過來點餐。

W：沒問題的，女士。在點餐前，需要喝點什麼嗎？

T：那不錯。我想團員們都口渴了。請給我們一些水及檸檬汁。

W：沒問題，女士。我等等將飲料送過去。

T：非常謝謝你。

W：您別客氣，女士。若您有需要協助的地方，請讓我知道。

T：是的，我發現有些團員沒有叉子和餐巾，可以請您幫我們拿過來嗎？

W：很抱歉，女士。我們馬上送過去。

單字 Vocabulary

1. **introduce** *v.* 介紹
   例 My boyfriend introduced his parent to me this morning.
   我男朋友今天早上介紹他的父母給我認識。

2. **delicious** *adj.* 美味的
   例 To have a delicious moon cake is a tradition in Taiwan to celebrate the Mid-Autumn Festival.
   在台灣，在中秋節吃美味的月餅是一項傳統。

3. **discuss** *v.* 討論
   例 We need to discuss whether to work with them or not again.
   我們還需再討論是否要和他們合作一事。

4. **shortly** *adv.* 立刻、馬上
   例 Mary is going to Brazil shortly.
   瑪莉即將要到巴西了。

Unit 04

4.4 換句話說 In Other Words

Would you like to have something to drink?

您想要喝點什麼嗎？

What would you like to drink first?

您想要先喝點什麼嗎？

Anything to drink?

您想要喝點什麼嗎？

What beverage would you like to drink?

您想要喝什麼飲料？

What would you like to order now?

您想要點什麼餐呢？

May I take your order now?

請問您要點餐了嗎？

Are you ready to order now?

請問您要點餐了嗎？

May I take an order for you now?

請問您要點餐了嗎？

You can select one of our four signature sauces at the bottom of the menu on page three.

您可以搭配其中一種我們的招牌醬料，在第三頁菜單的下方。

Our restaurant provides four sauces for your selection. Please see page three.

我們餐廳提供四種醬料，請翻到第三頁。

There are four signature sauces you can choose. Please refer to page three.

我們有四種招牌醬料供您選擇，請參考第三頁。

Please turn to page three. There are four signature sauces and you can choose one of them for your steak.

請翻到第三頁，這裡有四種招牌醬料，您可以為您的牛排挑選一個口味。

Could you briefly introduce what you have on the menu for us?

請你為我們簡單介紹一下菜單，好嗎？

We have no ideas about the dishes. Could you give us a brief introduciton?

我們對於點菜沒什麼想法，你可以簡單介紹一下嗎？

What is the signature dish in the restaurant?

你們的招牌菜是什麼？

I need recommendations. What do you recommend?

我需要推薦。你推薦什麼呢？

Unit 05 上菜服務 Serving Dishes

5.1 情境對話——和商務客的應答
Dialogue with Business Customers

 Track 13

 Waiter 服務生，簡稱 W。

 Guest, Mr. Brown 商務客，Brown 先生，簡稱 G。

W: Here is your Original Baby Back Ribs with original sauce.

G: Thank you. They look great; I'm so hungry now.

W: You're welcome, sir. And here is **Seared** Tuna for you, sir.

G: I don't think I've ordered this.

W: Let me check. We don't think we made any **mistakes**, sir. This is the dish you have ordered.

G: No, I'm sure I have not ordered this dish. There must be some **misunderstanding**. I **remember** I ordered the Smoked Tuna

With White Wine. Can I have it changed?

W: Certainly, sir. I apologize for the mistake.

G: It's Ok.

W: The dish takes quite some time to get ready. Can I get you anything first?

G: I would like to have an appetizer and drinks before the meal is ready.

W: Sure, no problem, sir. We will be back with the appetizer and two cups of coffee right away. Sorry for the mistake, again.

Unit 05

中文翻譯

W：這是您的經典嫩烤豬肋排佐，搭配原味經典佐醬。

G：謝謝你。看起來很美味，我現在超餓的。

W：您別客氣，先生。這是您的香煎鮪魚，先生。

G：我好像不是點這道菜。

W：讓我看看。沒有錯，先生，您是點這道菜。

G：不是，我很確定我不是點這道菜。或許是有些誤會了，我記得我點煙燻鮪魚佐白酒。請問我可以換嗎？

W：可以的，先生。很抱歉弄錯了。

G：沒關係。

W：餐點需要點時間料理。請問我能先上些什麼給您嗎？

G：在餐點準備好前，我想要來一份開胃菜和飲料。

W：沒問題，先生。開胃菜和兩杯咖啡馬上來。再次抱歉上錯菜。

單字 Vocabulary

1. **seared** *adj.* 香煎的

   例 I would like to have my tuna seared with white wine.
   我想要來份香煎鮪魚佐白酒。

2. **mistake** *n.* 錯誤、過失

   例 The city mayor apologized for his mistake caused by the metro construction.
   市長為了捷運建造工程的過失道歉。

3. **misunderstanding** *n.* 誤會、誤解

   例 The misunderstanding is made by the language barrier.
   語言隔閡造成了誤解。

4. **remember** *n.* 記得

   例 Tony is a real man now; I still remember he was a little boy since the first time I met him.
   湯尼現在是個男人了，我還記得我第一次見到他時，他還是個小男孩呢。

5.2 情境對話——和家庭客的應答
Dialogue with Family Guests

 Track 14

 Waiter 服務生，簡稱 W。

 Guest, Mr. Brown 家庭客，Brown 先生，簡稱 G。

W: Here are your Red Hot Buffalo Wings and Mozzarella Cheese for appetizer. Caesar Salad and Baked Potato Soup.

G: Wow, thank you! They look so **delicious**.

W: And here are two New York Steaks medium rare.

G: Thank you.

W: And here is Cheeseburger for the little **gentleman**.

G: Thank you.

W: All of your dishes have been served. Is there anything else I can get for you, sir?

G: Oh, yes. Please give me some **napkins**. And wait, is that pepper on the Cheeseburger? I'm afraid....

W: No, it's our special sauce. It's not pepper. Sorry for the misunderstanding.

G: No, not at all. We just want to double check since my kid will have allergic reactions to pepper.

W: Yes, we understand that, sir. To **seek** the balance between the best taste and guests' health, we have taken years developing various dishes to meet different needs.

G: **It's very thoughtful of you.** We knew your restaurant is one of the best in town.

W: Thank you for your support. And about the napkin, I'll bring it to you later. Enjoy your meal.

Unit 05

中文翻譯

W：這是您的開胃菜－香辣水牛城雞翅及摩扎瑞拉起司。凱薩沙拉及烤馬鈴薯濃湯。

G：哇，謝謝你。看起來很美味。

W：還有這是您的兩份三分熟牛排。

G：謝謝你。

W：還有這是給小紳士的起司漢堡。

G：謝謝你。

W：您的餐點都到齊了。您還有什麼需要點餐的嗎？

G：噢，有的。請給我一些餐巾紙。等等，起司漢堡上的是胡椒粉嗎？

W：不是，那是我們特製醬料，不是胡椒粉，很抱歉造成您的誤解。

G：不會的，我們只是想再次確認，因為我們的孩子對胡椒粉過敏。

W：是的，我們了解。為了能在口味和顧客的健康間取得平衡，我們花了很多年研發各種菜色，滿足不同的需求。

G：謝謝您們的用心，我們知道這裡是鎮上最好的餐廳。

W：感謝您的支持。餐巾我們等會就送上。用餐愉快。

單字 Vocabulary

1. **delicious** *adj.* 美味的

   例 Italy is famous for delicious desserts and sweets.
   義大利以美味的甜點與甜食聞名。

2. **gentleman** *n.* 紳士

   例 To be a gentleman, the first thing is to pay attention to your manner.
   當一個紳士，首先要注意的就是禮儀。

3. **napkin** *n.* 餐巾紙

   例 The waiter forgot bringing me some napkin as I asked for earlier.
   服務生忘記提供我先前要求的餐巾紙。

4. **seek** *v.* 尋找

   例 We need to seek for a possible solution to this problem.
   我們需要為這個問題尋求可能的解決之道。

5. **It's very thoughtful of you.** *ph.* 您人真好。（用於形容對方很體貼。）

   例 Thank you for giving me a hand just in time. It's very thought of you.
   感謝您即時給我的幫助，您真的很體貼。

5.3 情境對話——和團體客導遊的應答
Dialogue with Tour Guides

Track 15

 *Waiter，簡稱 **W**。*

 *Tour Guide, Ms. Brown 導遊，Brown 小姐，簡稱 **T**。*

 *Tourist 遊客，簡稱 **T**。*

W: Madam, the dishes are ready to **serve**.

T: Ok, thank you.

The waiter is starting to serve the meal to the group.

W: Here are Milano's Dinner Salad and French Onion Soup.
Would you like to have a lobster and rib **combo** now or later?

T: Now, please. We just can't wait.

W: Ok.

Two minutes later...

W: Here are Live Lobster & Rib Combo for you two, sir and
madam. And here are South Miami Fried Shrimp for you three.

T: Thank you. They look so delicious.

W: The two sauces next to the plate are for Lobster and Shrimp. You **definitely** have to try it.

T: Ok, I get it.

W: And here are water and lemonade. Anything else I can get for you?

T: Yes, we would like to have some red wine and some new napkins.

W: Sure, I'll be back with them for you soon.

T: Thank you.

W: You're welcome, madam. Enjoy your meal.

中文翻譯

W：女士，餐點已經準備好，可以上菜了。

T：好的，謝謝你。

餐廳服務生開始為旅遊團旅客送上餐點。

W：這是招牌沙拉及法式洋蔥湯。您要現在還是稍會送上新鮮龍蝦與肋排組合餐呢？

T：現在，謝謝。

W：好的。

兩分鐘後……

W：這是先生及女士的新鮮龍蝦與肋排組合餐。這是三位的邁阿密炸蝦。

T：謝謝你，看起來如此美味。

W：盤子旁的這兩種醬料是用來沾龍蝦和蝦子的，一定要吃吃看喔。

T：好的。

W：還有這是開水與檸檬汁。請問還有需要什麼嗎？

T：是的，我們想來些紅酒和餐巾紙。

W：好的，我盡快送過來給您。

T：謝謝。

W：您別客氣，女士。祝您用餐愉快。

單字 Vocabulary

1. **serve** *n.* 提供、供應

   例 The waiter served me a cup of coffee.
   服務生給我端上一杯咖啡。

2. **combo** *n.* 組合

   例 I would like to order a French fries and cheese burger combo.
   我想要點一份薯條及起司漢堡組合餐。

3. **definitely** *adv.* 相當、頗

   例 Trust me. It's definitely a must buy if you go to Japan.
   相信我，這絕對是去日本必買的商品。

5.4 換句話說 In Other Words

Is there anything else I can get for you?

請問還有需要什麼嗎？

Need anything else?

有需要什麼嗎？

Can I get you anything else?

我能替您拿些什麼嗎？

Do you need anything else?

你還需要其什麼嗎？

The dish takes quite some time to get ready. Can I get you anything first?

餐點需要點時間準備。請問您還需要什麼嗎？

It takes time to cook the dishes. Is there anything I can get for you?

餐點準備需要花點時間。有什麼需要我給您什麼嗎？

It will take about ten minutes to prepare the dish. Would you like anything to eat while waiting?

準備餐點需要花十分鐘的時間。趁餐點還沒來，您有想先吃點什麼嗎？

Would you like to have some appetizers while waiting for your dish? It may take some time.

您有想要在餐點來之前先吃點前菜嗎？這可能會花一些時間。

I don't think I've ordered this.

我好像不是點這道菜。

☕ **This is not the dish I ordered.**
這不是我點的菜。

☕ **There may be some misunderstanding about this order.**
關於點餐，可能有些誤會。

☕ **I got the wrong dish. Please check it.**
菜上錯了，請確認一下。

Can I have it changed?

請問我可以換嗎？

☕ **May I change my dish?**
我可以換我的餐嗎？

☕ **I got the wrong dish and I would like to change another.**
菜上錯了，我想換別的。

☕ **May I have another dish to exchange the wrong one?**
我可以點其他的菜來換這個上錯的菜嗎？

Unit 06 隨桌服務
Table Services

6.1 情境對話——和商務客的應答
Dialogue with Business Customers

 Track 16

 Waiter 服務生，簡稱 W。

 Guest, Mr. Brown 商務客，Brown 先生，簡稱 G。

W: Excuse me, sir. May I refill your glass?

G: Sure, please.

W: And do you like your meal tonight?

G: Yes. They are great. I love the **ribs** so much. Could you give me some **original** sauce?

W: Sure. I'll get that for you **shortly**. Is there anything I can get for you, sir?

G: Please give me another **fork** and some napkins.

W: Yes, sir. I'll be back with them soon.

G: Thank you.

Later...

W: Here is the original sauce for you. Would you like more oat bread?

G: No, thanks.

W: And here are your fork and napkins, sir.

G: Thank you.

W: You're welcome, sir. Did you drop this? **(pointing the coat on the floor)**

G: Yes, it's mine. Thank you. **(crouching and going to pick it up)**

W: Let me to help you with that. Do you mind if I hang your coat at the counter, sir?

G: That will be great, thank you.

Unit 06

中文翻譯

W：不好意思，請問需要幫您續杯嗎？

G：好的，麻煩了。

W：請問餐點都還可以嗎？

G：非常好，我超喜歡肋排的。請問可以再給我一點經典原味佐料嗎？

W：當然可以，我稍會兒拿給您。請問還有需要別的嗎，先生？

G：請給我叉子和一些餐巾。

W：好的，先生。我稍會兒過來。

G：謝謝你。

過了一會兒……

W：這是您的經典原味佐醬。請問您要再來一些麵包嗎？

G：不用了，謝謝。

W：這是您的叉子和餐巾，先生。

G：謝謝你。

W：您別客氣，先生。這是您掉的嗎？（指地上的外套……）

G：對，這是我的。（彎腰要撿……）

W：讓我來。您介意我幫您把您的外套放在櫃台嗎？

G：好啊，謝謝。

單字 Vocabulary

1. **rib** *n.* 肋排

   例 You have to taste the smoked ribs which are famous in this city or you can't say you have visited it.

   必須要去嚐看看這個城市很有名的碳烤豬肋排，否則別說你有來造訪過這座城市。

2. **original** *adj.* 最初的、原味的

   例 There are four kinds of flavors that the burger shop provides, but I like the original flavor the most.

   那間漢堡店提供四種風味的漢堡，但我最喜歡原味口味的。

3. **shortly** *adv.* 立刻、馬上

   例 Please wait me for a second; I'll be back shortly.

   請稍等我一下，我馬上回來。

4. **fork** *n.* 叉子

   例 The fork is made in Italy and really expensive.

   這支叉子是義大利製的，非常昂貴。

6.2 情境對話──和家庭客的應答
Dialogue with Family Guests

 Track 17

Waiter 服務生，簡稱 W。

Guest, Mr. Brown 家庭客，Brown 先生，簡稱 G。

G: Excuse me.

W: Yes, sir. How may I help you?

G: I would like to have some apple pies.

W: Sure, anything else I can get for you?

G: Please refill the coke for my son, thank you.

W: No problem, sir. Do you like the meal?

G: Yes, the buffalo wings are so spicy; I really like it. But the steaks are overcooked.

W: I'm so sorry. I'll take them back to the kitchen and get you another steak.

G: Thank you. By the way, please get me some ketchup.

W: Sure, sir. I'll get the ketchup for you in a minute.

G: Could we still order other dishes now?

W: That's for sure. What do you like to order?

G: We haven't decided it yet. Could we take a look of the menu again?

W: No problem. I'll be back with ketchup and the menu right away.

G: Thank you so much. Oh, sorry, one more thing. Could we get some water as well?

W: Ok. Please wait a second.

Unit 06

中文翻譯

G：不好意思。

W：是的，先生？請問有什麼需要幫忙的嗎？

G：我想要再來一些蘋果派。

W：當然可以，請問還需要別的嗎？

G：請幫我兒子續杯可樂，謝謝。

W：沒問題的，先生。餐點都還合您口味嗎？

G：是的，水牛城雞翅辣得很夠味，我真的很喜歡。但是牛排有點過熟了。

W：我很抱歉，我請廚房拿回去，再做一份新的給您。

G：謝謝。對了，請幫我拿點蕃茄醬過來。

W：當然，先生。我馬上幫您送番茄醬過來。

G：請問還能加點嗎？

W：好啊，您想加點什麼呢？

G：我們還沒確定，可以再看一下菜單嗎？

W：好的，番茄醬和菜單等下就送來。

G：謝謝您，噢對了，不好意思，我們還能要水嗎？

W：好的，等一下。

單字 Vocabulary

1. **overcooked** *adj.* 烹煮過熟的
   例 Because the chef didn't notice the time, the beef was overcooked.
   因為廚師沒有注意時間，所以牛肉煮過熟了。

2. **ketchup** *n.* 番茄醬
   例 Kids love French fries with ketchup.
   孩子們喜歡薯條配上番茄醬。

6.3 情境對話——和團體客導遊的應答
Dialogue with Tour Guides

 Track 18

 Waiter，簡稱 W。

 Tour Guide, Ms. Brown 導遊，Brown 小姐，簡稱 T。

 Tourist, Elisa 遊客，Elisa 小姐，簡稱 T。

W: Excuse me, madam. May I **refill** your **glass**?

T: Yes, please.

W: How is dinner for you?

T: It's so delicious. My group said that they would like to order some pasta and seafood combos.

W: No problem, madam. I'll take your order later.

T: Thank you.

W: How is your dish, madam?

T: The seafood is so great. I've never had the seafood like this.

W: Before serving the dessert, can I clean up all the plates and crumbs from the table?

T: Yes, please.

W: You're welcome, madam. I'll get the desserts for you later.

T: Excuse me. We also need tables over here cleaned.

W: Sure. We will get it done right away.

While the table is being cleaned up, one of tourists' water spilled out over the table.

T: Oh, sorry.

W: Don't worry. Here is the napkin for you. We will get you another glass of water later.

T: Thank you so much.

Unit 06

中文翻譯

W：不好意思，女士，請問我可以幫您續杯嗎？

T：好的，麻煩了。

W：餐點還可以嗎？

T：餐點非常美味。我的團員們還想點些義大利麵及海鮮組合。

W：沒問題，女士。我稍會兒過來為您點餐。

T：謝謝。

W：女士，您的餐點還可以嗎？

T：海鮮很棒。我從來沒嚐過像這樣的海鮮。

W：在為您送上甜點前，請問我可以替您收拾盤子及清理桌上的麵包屑嗎？

T：好的，麻煩了。

W：您別客氣，女士。我稍會兒為您送上甜點。

T：不好意思，這裡的桌子也要清理。

W：好的，馬上來。

服務生於清理桌子時，其中一位團員的水灑到滿桌子都是。

T：很抱歉。

W：別擔心，這是您的餐巾。等下會把新的水給您。

T：非常謝謝您。

單字 Vocabulary

1. **refill** *v.* 填滿、續杯
   例 I would like to have my drink refilled.
   我想要續杯我的飲料。

2. **glass** *n.* 玻璃、杯子
   例 My brother just broke my favorite glass.
   我弟弟剛打破我心愛的杯子。

3. **clean up** *v.* 清理
   例 It's a custom to clean up the house before the Chinese New Year.
   於新年前清理房屋是習慣。。

4. **crumb** *n.* 屑、麵包屑
   例 The waiter removed the crumbs on the table and cleaned it up.
   服務生將桌上的麵包屑清除並將桌子清理乾淨。

6.4 換句話說 In Other Words HELLO

I'll get that for you shortly.

我待會兒替您送上來。

🍵 **I'll get it for you right away.**

我待會兒替您送上來。

🍵 **I'll get it for you in a minute.**

我待會兒替您送上來。

🍵 **I'll get that for you at once.**

我待會兒替您送上來。

May I refill your glass?

我可以為您續杯飲料嗎？

🍵 **May I pour you a drink?**

我可以為您續杯飲料嗎？

🍵 **Would you like to have a refill?**

我可以為您續杯飲料嗎？

🍵 **May I get your glass and refill it?**

方便我拿您的杯子續杯嗎？

Could you give me some original sauce?

請問可以再給我一點經典原味佐料嗎？

May I have some original sauce?
我可以來些原味佐料嗎？

I would like to have another sauce. Would you bring me some?
我想要別的醬料，你可以拿一些給我嗎？

Please bring me some original sauce. Thank you.
請給我原味醬料。

Before serving the dessert, can I clean up all the plates and crumbs from the table?

在為您送上甜點前，請問我可以替您收拾盤子及清理桌上的麵包屑嗎？

May I clean the table for you before the dessert?
在送上甜點前，我可以為您清理桌面嗎？

Excuse me, sir. I need to clean up the plates and mob the table before serving the dessert.
先生，不好意思。在送上甜點前，我將要先收走盤子及清理桌面。

Please let me clean the table for you before serving the dessert.
請讓我再為您送上甜點前清理桌面。

Unit
07
結帳送客
May / Could I have the check, please?

7.1
情境對話──和商務客的應答
Dialogue with Business Customers

 Track 19

 Waiter 服務生，簡稱 W。

 Guest, Mr. Brown 商務客，Brown 先生，簡稱 G。

G: Could I have my **check**, please?

W: Yes, sir. I'll take it right back to you.

After a while...

W: Sir, here you are.

G: Ok, may I pay now?

W: Sure. How would you like to pay?

G: We would like to pay at once, please.

W: Ok, sir. That is $2,550 altogether, including 10% service charge. How would you like to make a **payment**?

G: Do you take a credit card?

W: Yes, sir. May I have your card, please?

G: Sure.

W: I'll be back shortly.

Later...

W: Sir, here is your receipt.

G: Thank you.

W: I hope you like the meal tonight.

G: Yes, we like it. It was great.

W: Thank you! Hope to see you soon, sir.

Unit 07

中文翻譯

G：請把帳單給我,謝謝?

W：好的,先生。我稍會兒將帳單拿給您。

過一會兒……

W：先生,您的帳單。

G：好的,我想要結帳了。

W：好的。您想要怎麼付帳呢?

G：一次結清就好,麻煩了。。

W：好的,先生。包含 10% 服務費,總共是 2,550 元。請問您要使用怎
　　麼樣的付款方式呢?

G：可以使用信用卡嗎?

W：可以的,先生。請提供我您的信用卡。

G：當然。

W：我很快就回來。

稍後……

W：先生，這是您的收據。

G：謝謝你。

W：我希望餐點您會喜歡。

G：是的，餐點很棒。

W：謝謝您。希望可以很快再與您相見，先生。

單字 Vocabulary

1. **check** *n.* 帳單（英式：bill，但餐廳英語較長使用 check）

   例1 May I have the check, please?
   我可以結帳了嗎？

   例2 The poor old man has no money to pay for his utility bill.
   那個窮困的老先生沒有錢來付清他的水電費帳單。

2. **payment** *n.* 付帳

   例 You can make a payment by ATM.
   您可用自動櫃員機付帳。

7.2 情境對話——和家庭客的應答
Dialogue with Family Guests

 Track 20

*Waiter 服務生，簡稱 **W**。*

*Guest, Mr. Brown 家庭客，Brown 先生，簡稱 **G**。*

The waiter standing next to the table finds his guest is looking around. So he comes around to ask if the guest needs anything...

W: Do you need to have the bill now?

G: Yes, please.

W: Here is the bill. The total fee is $1,050.

G: Is there any service charge included?

W: Yes, the 10% service charge is already included, sir.

G: Well, I think there is a mistake. I don't think we have ordered that. Could you please **check** the list again?

W: No problem, sir. Let me check the bill, please wait.

G: Sure.

W: Yes, sir. You are right. I apologize for the mistake.

G: It doesn't matter.

W: How would you like to pay?

G: Cash, please. Wait a moment. Your Ribs tonight are great. I think I would like to have one more portion for that. Sorry for bringing it up till now.

W: It's fine. But it takes time to get that ready. Do you mind if you make a payment now?

G: Ok.

W: Sure, it is $950 altogether, **including** the service charge. Here is your **receipt**. Sir, before you have your takeout, you can take a seat here.

G: Ok. Thank you.

W: Sir, here is your takeout. Spicy Ribs.

G: Ok. Thank you again.

Unit 07

中文翻譯

站在桌旁的服務生發現他的顧客左顧右盼，因此他上前詢問他是否有任何
需要⋯⋯

W：您現在要結帳了嗎？

G：是的，麻煩了。

W：這是您的帳單。總共是 1,050 元。

G：這有包含服務費了嗎？

W：是的，已經包含 10% 的服務費了，先生。

G：嗯，我認為這金額錯了。我想我們應該沒有點貴點的東西。請你再幫
我確認一下帳單好嗎？

W：沒問題，先生。讓我為您查一下，請稍等。

G：當然好的。

W：是的，先生，您沒有錯。我為這個錯誤向您道歉。

G：沒關係。

W：您想要用怎麼樣的付款方式呢？

G：現金麻煩了。您的肋排好吃極了，我想我還要一份，很抱歉現在才提
起。

W：沒關係的，但烹煮還需要一些時間，您介意先付款嗎？

G：好的。

W：好的，包含服務費，總共是 950 元。這是您的發票。先生，在等您的外帶的期間，請您在這裡稍坐。

G：好的，謝謝您。

W：這是您外帶的辣味肋排。

G：好的，謝謝。

單字 Vocabulary

1. **check** *v.* 核對

   例 Could you please check the details of the sheet before sending it to the outsiders?

   可以請你在送出表單給外界使用者時，檢查一下表單內容嗎？

2. **include** *v.* 包含、包括

   例 The sale tax is not included in the selling price, so you have to pay it additionally.

   銷售稅沒有含在銷售價格裡，所以你必須額外支付它。

3. **receipt** *n.* 發票

   例 The customer checked the receipt after paying.

   顧客於付款後，核對了一下收據。

7.3 情境對話──和團體客導遊的應答
Dialogue with Tour Guides

 Track 21

 Waiter，簡稱 W。

 Tour Guide, Ms. Brown 導遊，Brown 小姐，簡稱 T。

T: Excuse me. May I have our check, please?

W: Yes, madam. I'll get the bill for you, please wait.

After a while...

W: Here you are. Would you like to pay at the **cashier** or let me help you?

T: Now, please. Thank you.

W: No problem. It is $5,690 **altogether**, including 10% service charge. How would you like to make a payment?

T: Can I pay by debit card?

W: I'm sorry, madam. We don't take debit card; we only accept cash and credit cards.

T: Ok.

W: Here is the **receipt** for you. How was the meal? Was it great?

T: Yes, it was great. Hope we can come and enjoy the meal again soon. By the way, is it ok for us to get some more desserts? Some of the group members told me they like them very much and want to have some when they are back to the hotel.

W: Sure, which dessert would you like to have?

T: Tiramisu. We need a couple of Tiramisu, please. And here is the money for the dessert.

W: Ok, I will bring the receipt and Tiramisu for you later.

Five minutes later...

W: Here are your receipt and Tiramisu.

T: Thank you so much.

W: You are welcome, madame. We are glad that you all liked the meal tonight. We look forward to seeing you next time soon!

Unit 07

中文翻譯

T：不好意思，可以幫我拿帳單過來嗎？

W：好的，女士。我稍會兒為您奉上帳單，請稍等。

過了一會兒……

W：這是您的帳單。您想要到櫃檯結帳或是由我來替您服務呢？

T：現在付款，麻煩了。

W：沒問題。包含 10% 服務費，總共是 5,690 元。請問您要使用怎麼樣的付款方式呢？

T：我可以使用支票卡嗎？

W：不好意思，女士。我們不提供使用支票卡，我們只有接受使用現金及信用卡。

T：好的。

W：這是您的收據。請問餐點如何呢？您覺得不錯嗎？

T：是的，餐點很不錯。希望我們可以很快地再來品嚐美食。對了，我們還能點些甜點嗎？我們的團員告訴我他們非常喜歡您們的甜點，回飯店後還想吃。

W：沒問題，請問您想要的甜點是什麼？

T：提拉米蘇，我們要一打的提拉米蘇，這裡是甜點的費用。

W：好的，待會會將收據和甜點送上來。

五分鐘後……

W：這是您的收據和甜點。

T：謝謝您。

W：別客氣，我很開心您與您的賓客都喜歡。期待下次可以很快地再次
與您相見！

單字 Vocabulary

1. **cashier** *n.* 出納
   例 The auto cashier now is popular in some supermarkets.
   自動化結帳現在在某些超市很流行。

2. **altogether** *adv.* 總共
   例 She bought the whole warehouse and the equipment for her new business altogether.
   她為了她的新事業總共買了整個廠房及設備。

3. **receipt** *n.* 收據
   例 The receipt showed all the items that you bought in details.
   收據上面顯示所有你購買的商品明細。

7.4 換句話說 In Other Words

Do you need to have the bill now?

您現在要結帳了嗎？

 Would you like to pay now?

請問您要結帳了嗎？

Do you want to have the bill?

請問您需要帳單明細嗎？

Would you like to have the bill now?

請問您需要帳單明細嗎？

Could I have my check, please?

請把帳單給我，謝謝？

We would like to have the check now, please.

結帳！

I would like to have my check now.

我想要結帳。

Please bring me the check.

請拿帳單給我。

How would you like to make a payment?

請問您要使用怎麼樣的付款方式呢？

How would you like to pay?

您想怎麼付款呢？

Would you like to pay by cash or by credit card?

您想用現金或信用卡付款呢？

Would you mind if I take your credit card first?

您介意我先拿您的信用卡嗎？

Is there any service charge included?

這有包含服務費了嗎？

Any service fees included?

有包含服務費嗎？

Does the price include the service charge?

價格裡有含服務費嗎？

Should I pay the additional service fee?

我需要付額外的服務費嗎？

Unit 07

Unit
08
處理顧客抱怨
Dealing with Complaints

8.1 情境對話——和商務客的應答
Dialogue with Business Customers *Track 22*

 Waiter 服務生，簡稱 W。

 Guest, Mr. Brown 商務客，Brown 先生，簡稱 G。

W: Something wrong here, sir?

G: Yes. I have ordered a well-done steak. But, you see, it's medium rare here.

W: I'm so sorry, sir. I'll **return** it back to the kitchen and then bring you another steak well cooked. Please wait.

The waiter takes the steak back. Five minutes later, he brings the well-done steak to Mr. Brown.

W: Sir, here is your steak.

G: Thank you.

W: Is it ok?

G: Yes, it's good this time.

W: I'm glad you like it. And here we have some drinks for you to enjoy with the steak. They're free of charge to show our apology.

G: Thank you.

W: I hope you enjoy the meal.

A while later...

G: Excuse me.

W: Yes, sir. What can I do for you?

G: I have asked one of your waiters to get my water refilled. But somehow I have kept waiting for a while. I think he forgot it.

W: Sorry, sir. The house is a bit busy during the dinner time. We are sorry for that. I will get your water refilled now.

G: Ok. Thank you.

Unit 08

中文翻譯

W：先生，怎麼了嗎？

G：是的。我剛點的牛排是要全熟的，但你看，這邊是三分熟的。

W：我很抱歉，先生。我會將這份退回廚房，在幫您弄一份全熟的牛排過來，請您稍等。

餐廳服務生將牛排退回。五分鐘過後，他送來一份全熟的牛排給 Brown 先生。

W：先生，您的牛排來了。

G：謝謝你。

W：還可以嗎？

G：是的，這次很棒。

W：我很高興您喜歡。還有這是一些招待您享用牛排時，搭配飲用的飲品。為表示本飯店的歉意，這是免費招待給您的。

G：謝謝你。

W：祝您享用愉快。

一陣子過後……

G：不好意思。

W：是的，我能為您做些什麼嗎？

G：我詢問過您們的一位服務生，請他幫我重新裝水。但我不知道為什麼等了好久，我想他是忘了。

W：抱歉，先生。餐廳在晚餐時間都會比較忙。我很抱歉，我現在就幫您重新裝水。

G：好的，謝謝您。

單字 Vocabulary

1. **return** v. 送回、歸還
   例 The missing jewelry was returned to the luxury shop by an old lady.
   這件遺失的珠寶由一位老太太送回到精品店。

2. **show** v. 表示
   例 In order to show the respect for the soldiers sacrificed during the war, they built a memorial hall in the center of the city.
   為了對在戰爭中犧牲的士兵們表示尊敬，他們在市中心建造了一座紀念堂。

Unit 08

8.2 情境對話──和家庭客的應答
Dialogue with Family Guests

 Track 23

 Waiter 服務生，簡稱 W。

 Guest, Mr. Brown 家庭客，Brown 先生，簡稱 G。

G: Excuse me.

W: Yes, sir? How may I help you?

G: I have been waiting my meal for almost half an hour.

W: I'm so sorry, sir. I'll check it right now.

G: Ok.

After a while...

W: I'm so sorry, sir. I just checked your order with the chef; the meal was wrongly served to another table. I'll get you another meal later. I apologize for our carelessness.

G: That's ok.

W: Here are some appetizers for you and some potato chips and crackers for your kids. The appetizers and snacks will not be charged. They are on the house.

G: Thanks.

Five minute later...

G: Excuse me. How come we still haven't got our meal? I don't think we want to have that anymore. (standing up...)

W: Sorry sir. Please wait. You meal will be here right away. We're truly sorry about that. The house is usually busy this time.

Serving the meal...

W: Sir, here are your French fried shrimp and chicken risotto combo and Cheese burger. I apologize for the delay again. Hope you enjoy the meal this time. And don't forget to use snacks for free.

G: What do you have for the snacks?

W: Fruit cakes and apple pies. The apples are particularly fresh for this season. Please do try some later.

G: Ok, thank you.

Unit 08

中文翻譯

G：不好意思。

W：是的，先生？請問有哪邊需要幫忙的嗎？

G：我等餐點已經等了大概半小時了。

W：我很抱歉，先生。我幫您確認一下。

G：好的。

過了一陣子……

W：我很抱歉，先生。我剛才幫您跟廚師確認了，您的餐點誤送到別桌客人那裡了。我等一下會幫您送一份過來。對於我們失誤的地方，我很抱歉。

G：沒關係。

W：這是一些招待您的開胃菜及一些招待您小孩的薯片、餅乾。這些是不需要付費的，由本餐廳招待。

G：謝謝。

五分鐘過後……

G：不好意思，為什麼我們的餐點都還沒上？我想我們可以不用吃了（起身……）

W：先生，很抱歉，您的餐點馬上來。真的很抱歉，餐廳在這個時候都會比較忙。

上菜……

G：您們有什麼甜點呢？

W：水果蛋糕和蘋果派。這個季節的蘋果特別新鮮，請您一定要試試看。

G：好的，謝謝您。

W：先生，這是您的法式炸蝦及雞肉燉飯組合餐以及起司漢堡。延誤您的用餐時間，我再次與您道歉。希望您可以喜歡這次的餐點。

單字 Vocabulary

1. **carelessness** *n.* 草率、粗心大意
   例 The boy showed his apology for his carelessness.
   這男孩為了他的粗心大意道歉。

2. **cracker** *n.* （鹹）薄脆餅乾
   例 I like to have some crackers in the afternoon.
   我喜歡在下午的時候吃點餅乾。

3. **snack** *n.* 零食、零嘴
   例 Please buy some snacks when you're on the way home.
   在你回家的路上，請幫我買些零食。

4. **delay** *n.* 延遲
   例 It's raining cats and dogs outside. We can't deliver the package on time. Sorry for the dealy.
   現在外面正下著大雨，我們無法準時將包裹送達，對此延誤我們感到抱歉。

Unit 08

8.3 情境對話──和團體客導遊的應答
Dialogue with Tour Guides

 Track 24

 *Waiter，簡稱 **W**。*

 *Tour Guide, Ms. Brown 導遊，Brown 小姐，簡稱 **T**。*

 *Tourist, Ariel 遊客，Ariel 小姐，簡稱 **T**。*

W: Something wrong here, madam?

T: Yes. I don't think we have ordered the seafood combo.

W: Let me check it for you, madam. Please wait.

T: Sure.

One minute later...

W: Madam, I apologize for the wrong serving. I'll return it back to the kitchen **immediately.**

T: Wait a second. She has a problem with her steak.

W: What's wrong with your steak, madam?

T: I want my steak medium rare. But this steak is almost medium well.

W: I'm so sorry about the steak. I'll get it fixed right away. What else can I do for you?

T: My daughter has an egg allergy. I reminded the waiter who took the order for us earlier. But her steak still has an egg on the top. Could you please change another one without eggs?

W: Ok, I'll change that for you, too. Sorry for the mistake, madam.

A few minutes later...

W: Here you go. I'm really sorry about this. How about the steak this time?

T: Pretty good.

W: Here is smoked tuna with mozzarella cheese for you. To show our apology, it's free of charge.

T: Thank you.

W: If there is anything we can help you with, please let us know. Enjoy your meal.

Unit 08

中文翻譯

W：女士，請問怎麼了嗎？

T：是的，我不認為我們有點海鮮組合餐。

W：讓我為您確認一下，女士。請稍等。

T：當然。

一分鐘過後……

W：女士，我為送錯餐點給您道歉。我立刻將餐點退回廚房。

T：等一下，她的牛排有些問題。

W：請問您的牛排有什麼問題呢，女士？

T：我點的牛排是三分熟，但這塊牛排幾乎是七分熟了。

W：我很抱歉，我馬上幫您處理。還有需要幫忙的地方嗎？

T：我的女兒對蛋過敏。我有提醒過剛剛幫我們點餐的服務生了。可是現在牛排上還有蛋。請問您能幫我換沒有蛋的嗎？

W：沒問題，我也會幫您換。很抱歉，女士。

幾分鐘過後……

W：您的牛排來了。我感到非常抱歉。請問這次牛排還行嗎？

T：非常好。

W：這裡有些煙燻鮪魚佐摩扎瑞拉起司，是要招待您的。為表達我們的歉意，這是不需要付費的。

W：若還有我們能夠幫忙的地方，請讓我們知道。祝您用餐愉快。

單字 Vocabulary

1. **immediately** *adv.* 立即地、立刻地

   例 Please write it down immediately when you listen to the keyword from the radio.
   當你從錄音機聽到關鍵字時，請麻煩立刻寫下來。

2. **medium rare** *adj.* 三分熟

   例 I want my steak medium rare.
   我想要三分熟的牛排。

3. **almost** *adv.* 幾乎、差不多

   例 It was almost midnight when they arrived at the city.
   當他們抵達這座城市時幾乎已是午夜時間。

8.4 換句話說 In Other Words

Here is smoked tuna with mozzarella cheese for you. It's free of charge to show our apology.

這裡有些煙燻鮪魚佐摩扎瑞拉起司，是要招待您的。對於延誤您的用餐，為表達我們的歉意，這是不需要付費的。

🍵 **There are some smoked tuna with mozzarella cheese for free to represent our apology.**

這裡有些煙燻鮪魚佐摩扎瑞拉起司，是要招待您的。對於延誤您的用餐，為表達我們的歉意，這是不需要付費的。

🍵 **This smoked tuna with mozzarella cheese is free of charge to show our apology for getting your meal delayed.**

這裡有些煙燻鮪魚佐摩扎瑞拉起司，是要招待您的。對於延誤您的用餐，為表達我們的歉意，這是不需要付費的。

🍵 **This smoked tuna with mozzarella cheese is on the house to show our apology for the delay.**

這裡有些煙燻鮪魚佐摩扎瑞拉起司，是要招待您的。對於延誤您的用餐，為表達我們的歉意，這是不需要付費的。

I'll return it back to the kitchen and then bring you another steak well cooked. Please wait.

我會將這份退回廚房，在幫您弄一份全熟的牛排過來，請您稍等。

> I'll return the dish back to the chef, and it will take some time to cook a new one.

我將會把這份餐退回給廚師，會花點時間才能送上新的一份餐給您。

> I'll bring you a new well-cooked steak for you, and this one will be returned.

我等會兒再給您送上牛排，這份我要先退回去。

> It will take time to prepare a well-cooked dish for you. I'll return this one back to the kitchen and bring you some appetizers before the new one is done.

您的餐點重做需要花點時間。我將會先把這份退回廚房，趁餐點還沒做好前，先給您送上一些前菜。

I apologize for our carelessness.

對於我們失誤的地方，我很抱歉。

> I'm so sorry that the meal was wrongly served to another table.

我很抱歉送錯餐點。

> I apologize for the mistake.

我為我們的誤解向您道歉。

> It's our fault to make you feel uncomfortable. I apologize here.

讓您感到不舒服是我們的失誤，我在這邊跟您道歉。

Unit
09 其它
Others

9.1 情境對話──和商務客的應答
Dialogue with Business Customers

 Track 25

*Manager 餐廳經理，簡稱 **M**。*

*Guest, Mr. Brown 商務客，Brown 先生，簡稱 **G**。*

The manager is calling Mr. Brown, who left the questionnaire of customer satisfaction last evening and pointed out his discontent with the waitress' attitude.

M: Hello, may I speak to Mr. Brown?

G: Yes, this is Brown speaking. May I ask who's calling, please?

M: This is John Smith, the manager of Happy Friday Restaurant. I just **reviewed** the questionnaire that you filled out last evening and noticed that you were not satisfied with our services. May I inquire about what happened last evening?

G: Yes. My colleague and I had been waiting the meal for a long time; we asked the waitress to see if the meal is ready or not. The waitress seemed to be inattentive, so we asked her again. Then she yelled "Could you please just wait? It's almost done!" I don't like to be treated like that.

M: I apologize for her attitude. We will keep looking into this matter and have our service improved.

G: Yes, please. And about your restrooms, especially the lady's rooms, are not clean. The trash can is packed with toilet papers.

M: We're sorry for making you uncomfortable. We will send people to check the trash cans and keep the restrooms clean. We appreciate your opinions.

G: Ok, or I don't think I will go to your restaurant again. Actually it's quite a shock to me because it's a highly recommended restaurant in town.

M: We are truly sorry, again. In order to show our apology, we will provide you the luxury lobster and oyster combo free of charge.

G: OK.

中文翻譯

餐廳經理正打電話給 **Brown** 先生，因為昨晚 **Brown** 先生留下顧客滿意度調查表並指出他對於服務生的服務態度不滿意。

M：你好，請問我可以與 Brown 先生通話嗎？

G：是的，我是 Brown 先生。請問您哪邊？

M：我是 John Smith，快樂星期五餐廳的經理。我剛剛檢視您昨晚填寫的問卷表，得知您對於昨晚的服務不滿意。請問我可以知道昨晚發生了什麼事嗎？

G：可以。我同事與我昨天等餐點等了很久，我們詢問服務生幫我們確認餐點好了沒。服務生看起來心不在焉，，所以我們又再問了一次，然後她就對我們吼，說「你可以等一下嗎？就快好了啊！」我不喜歡那樣被對待。

M：我為這位服務生的態度向您道歉。我們會持續注意這件事，並改善我們的服務。

G：麻煩了。還有您的廁所，特別是女廁，很不乾淨。垃圾桶塞滿了衛生紙。

M：我們很抱歉讓您感到不適。我們會派人去檢查垃圾桶，並保持廁所乾淨。很感謝您給的意見。

G：好的，我想我不會再去這家餐廳了，事實上，我有點震驚，因為這是鎮上評價最高的餐廳。

M：我們真的很抱歉。為了表示我們的歉意，我們提供奢華龍蝦及生蠔組合套餐來招待您。

單字 Vocabulary

1. **questionnaire** *n.* 問卷
   例 The students designed a medical questionnaire to do research for their thesis.
   學生們為了他們的論文，設計醫學問卷來做研究。

2. **satisfaction** *n.* 滿意、稱心
   例 The boss smiled with satisfaction while seeing the net profit of the first quarter.
   老闆看到第一季淨獲利後，很滿意地笑著。

3. **discontent** *n.* 不滿
   例 Judy showed her discontent with the services of the hair salon she went this afternoon.
   Judy 對於下午她去的那間沙龍的服務很不滿意。

4. **review** *v.* 覆核、檢視
   例 The team in charge needs to review every document that her team members prepared.
   領組需要覆核每份由組員編制的文件。

   註：其它單字請詳見 9.2。

9.2 情境對話——和家庭客的應答
Dialogue with Family Guests

 Track 26

*Waiter 服務生，簡稱 **W**。*

*Guest, Mr. Brown 家庭客，Brown 先生，簡稱 **G**。*

Mr. Brown wants to book a table for the family party on Sunday evening at Happy Friday Restaurant to celebrate Mother's Day and he is going to call the restaurant for more information about the service hours.

W: Good evening, this is Happy Friday Restaurant. How may I help you?

G: Yes. I would like to know the service hours this Sunday?

W: Yes, sir. Our restaurant will start to serve at 11:00 AM, and our last order will be **extended** to 10:30 PM due to Mother's Day. We offer all-day long service every Sunday.

G: Are there any tables still available for about 11 people?

W: I'm afraid there are no tables available for 11 people. How about Saturday? We will begin the service at 9:00 AM for breakfast, or you can choose the lunch or dinner service as well. Our last order for lunch is 1:30 PM and 9:00 PM for dinner.

G: I see. I will think about it and then call back for booking. Thanks a lot.

W: You're welcome, sir.

The same guest is calling back again...

W: This is Happy Friday Restaurant. How may I help you?

G: I'd like to book a table for 11 people this Saturday. We want the table in the non-smoking area as well.

W: Ok, let me check it for you. Sorry sir, all the tables in the non-smoking are fully booked.

G: Oh. Ok, thank you.

W: We are sorry about that. Every time when Mother's Day is approaching, tables are usually reserved several weeks ahead. But we also offer some available tables for guests coming in person because there is still a chance that some reservations will be cancelled.

G: Ok, thank you for telling me about that. I will think about it.

中文翻譯

Brown 先生想要為他的家人於禮拜天晚間預定快樂星期五餐廳的席位，來慶祝母親節，所以他正要打電話詢問餐廳服務時間。

W：晚安您好，這裡是快樂星期五餐廳。很開心為您服務。

G：是的，我想知道星期天的服務時間。

W：是的，先生。本餐廳禮拜天將於早上十一點開始提供服務，因為母親節之緣故，最後點餐時間將延長至晚間十點半。每週日都是全天候服務。

G：那還有十一人的位子嗎？

W：我很抱歉沒有給十一人的位子了。請問週六如何？我們將於早上九點開始提供早餐服務，或是您可以選擇午餐或晚餐時間也可以。最後點餐時間，午餐是至下午一點半，晚餐是至晚上九點。

G：我瞭解了。我想一下，再打電話進來訂位。非常謝謝你。

W：您別客氣，先生。

同樣的客人又來電了……

W：這裡是星期五餐廳，很高興為您服務。

G：我想訂星期天 11 人的位置。位置要在非吸菸區。

W：好的，讓我為您查一下。先生，很抱歉，非吸菸區的位置都訂滿了。

G：喔，好的，謝謝您。

W：很抱歉。每次只要在快到母親節的時候，位置通常在幾個禮拜前都訂滿了。但我們也有提供位置給現場的客人，有些位置有可能會取消訂位。

G：謝謝您特地告訴我，我會再想想看的。

單字 Vocabulary

1. **inattentive** *adj.* 心不在焉
   例 Some inattentive mothers lost their kids in the supermarket.
   有些心不在焉的媽媽會把小孩弄丟在超級市場。

2. **luxury** *n.* 奢華、奢侈
   例 The family lives in luxury.
   這家人過得很奢華。

3. **extend** *v.* 延長
   例 The closing time today will be extended to 10:00 PM.
   今日結束營業時間將延長至 10 點。

9.3 情境對話——給顧客的通知
Notices to Customers

Dear Customers,

To provide the better services, we plan to conduct a routine **maintenance** for the kitchen facilities and **renovate** the restaurant from January 15 to March 2. The service will be **resumed** on March 3. We apologize for the inconvenience.

Thank you for being a **loyal** customer for such a long time. We surely will be back with a new look and service that impress all of you.

Looking forward to seeing and having you on the reopen day.

Sincerely,

Happy Friday Restaurant

Dear Customers,

To provide better foods and services, we are closed temporarily from March 15 to March 29 for having a routine staff training course. The service will be resumed on March 30. Sorry for the inconvenience.

For a long time, your support has been our greatest **encouragement**. We promise that we will be back with the best foods and services that will never let you down.

See you soon.

Sincerely,

Happy Friday Restaurant

中文翻譯

親愛的客戶，

　　為提供更好的服務，我們計劃於一月十五日至三月二日來維修廚房設施及重新裝修餐廳。重新開幕時間為三月三日，造成不便，請您見諒。

　　感謝您長久以來的支持，我們真的很期待重新開幕的那天可以與您相會。

　　由衷感謝

快樂星期五餐廳 致

親愛的顧客您好，

　　為了提供更好的餐點和服務，我們將於 3/15 至 3/29 參加例行的員工訓練課程，因此這段時間將暫時不營業，很抱歉為您帶來不便。

　　在這段期間，您的支持一直是我們最大的鼓勵。我們承諾將帶來更好的餐點與服務，絕對不讓您失望。

　　期待下次見。

　　由衷感謝

快樂星期五餐廳 致

單字 Vocabulary

1. **maintain** *v.* 維修、保養；**maintenance** *n.*
   例 Jason maintains his motorcycle very well.
   Jason 把他的摩托車保養地很好。

2. **renovate** *v.* 重新裝修
   例 The old house was renovated by the city government for the use of library.
   這舊房子被市政府重新裝修做為圖書館用途。

3. **resume** *n.* 重新開始
   例 The speech was resumed after it was interfered by a commotion.
   演說因騷動干擾打斷後，又再次重新開始。

4. **loyal** *adj.* 忠誠的
   例 He has been a loyal fan to this pop idol.
   他一直是這位流行偶像的死忠粉絲。

5. **encouragement** *n.* 鼓勵
   例 Everyone needs encouragement to keep going on.
   每個人都需要鼓勵來繼續下去。

9.4 換句話說 In Other Words

May I inquire about what happened last evening?

請問我可以知道昨晚發生什麼事嗎？

Could you tell me what happened last evening?

請問您可以告訴我昨晚發生什麼事嗎？

Could you tell me what was going on last evening?

請問您可以告訴我昨晚發生什麼事嗎？

May I ask you what has happened last evening?

請問您可以告訴我昨晚發生什麼事嗎？

I just reviewed the questionnaire that you filled out last evening and noticed that you were not satisfied with our services.

我剛剛檢視您昨晚填寫的問卷表，得知您對於昨晚的服務不滿意。

I would like to know whether our service meets your requirement last night.

我想知道，您對於我們昨晚的服務，是不是覺得沒有符合您的要求。

I read your questionnaire and noticed that there is something you are not happy about.

我看了您的問卷，得知您有不滿意的地方。

I would like to know if there were some misunderstandings that caused your discontent with our services.

我想要知道，是不是有些誤會，讓您對於我們的服務不滿意。

We'll keep looking into this matter and have our service improved.
我們會持續注意這件事，並改善我們的服務。

I'll deal with it and find the way out.
我會處理這件事，並找出解決方法。

I'll take over this problem, and will reply you with the answer.
我會接管這個問體，並且將會給您回覆。

The problem will be solved; please kindly wait for my reply.
這個問題會被解決，請等待我的回覆。

I'm afraid there are no tables available for 11 people. How about Saturday?
我很抱歉沒有給十一人的位子了。請問週六如何？

I'm so sorry that we don't have any available seats for a large party. Would you like to reserve another day?
我很抱歉，我們沒有給大團體的座位了。還是您想要預訂別的日期呢？

I apologize that we don't take reservation during the national holidays.
很抱歉，在國定假日我們不提供訂位。

Sorry, there are no available seats for the time you requested. How about the dinner time?
抱歉，沒有符合您要求的座位。還是您要選擇晚餐時段呢？

Unit
10 外送餐點
Food Delivery

10.1 情境對話——和商務客的應答
Dialogue with Business Customers

 Track 27

Waiter 服務生，簡稱 W。

Guest, Mr. Brown 商務客，Brown 先生，簡稱 G。

The phone is ringing.

W: Good afternoon, this is Happy Friday Restaurant. How may I help you?

G: Yes. I would like to order food **delivery**.

W: Yes, sir. I can take an order for you.

G: I found there is a **promotion** of **premium** business lunch set on the website now.

W: Yes, we provide three different main **courses** for premium business lunch; and the courses are Italian Risotto, Smoked Ribs and New York Steak.

G: Good. Then I would like to have five Italian Risotto, two Smoked Ribs and three New York Steak.

W: No problem, sir. Would you like some appetizers?

G: What do you recommend?

W: Our best-selling dish is mozzarella cheese with **fresh** tomato. Would you like some?

G: Yes, for two, please.

W: No problem, sir. May I have your name, phone number and the address so that we can deliver your order?

G: Sure. John Brown, 4569-9987. The address is No.34, West Madison Road.

W: Ok, sir. We will get your order ready. Thanks for calling. Good bye.

Unit 10

中文翻譯

電話鈴聲響起……

W：午安您好，這裡是快樂星期五餐廳。請問我可以為您效勞嗎？

G：是的，我想點外送餐點。

W：有的，先生。我可以為您點餐。

G：我看到網站上正在促銷豪華商業午餐。

W：有的，我們有提供三種不同主餐的商業午餐，義式燉飯、碳烤肋排及牛排。

G：太好了。那麼我想要五份義式燉飯、兩份碳烤肋排及三份牛排。

W：沒問題，先生。請問你需要來點開胃菜嗎？

G：你推薦什麼呢？

W：我們賣最好的是水牛起司搭配新鮮蕃茄。您想要來一點嗎？

G：好的，來兩份，麻煩了。

W：沒問題，先生。請提供您的名字、電話號碼及地址，以方便我們替您送餐？

G：當然可以，John Brown，4569-9987。地址是梅迪森西街三十四號。

W：好的，先生。我們將會備妥您的餐點，感謝您的來電，再見。

單字 Vocabulary

1. **delivery** *n.* 遞送、傳遞
   例 You can check the delivery process on the logistic company's website.
   你可以上物流公司網站查詢快遞的進度。

2. **promotion** *n.* 促銷、推銷
   例 They are making a big promotion for the new arrivals.
   他們正在為新上架的商品舉辦大型促銷活動。

3. **premium** *adj.* 高價的、優質的
   例 It's a premium class diamond, so the price is a little bit higher.
   這是比較等級比較高的鑽石，所以價格上稍微高一點。

4. **course** *n.* 一道菜
   例 The main course is baked sweet potato.
   主菜是烤地瓜。

10.2 情境對話——和家庭客的應答
Dialogue with Family Guests

 Track 28

Waiter 服務生，簡稱 W。

Guest, Mr. Brown 家庭客，Brown 先生，簡稱 G。

The phone is ringing.

W: Good afternoon, this is Mamamia Italian Pizzeria. How may I help you?

G: Yes. I would like to make a food delivery order, but I cannot find the menu on your website.

W: I'm sorry, sir. We just re-established our website. Please try this: www.mamamiaitaliapizza.com.

G: Ok, thank you. I'll call back later.

Five minutes later...

W: This is Mamamia Italian Pizzeria. How may I help you?

G: Yes, I would like to order food delivery.

W: Ok, sir. What kind of flavor would you like to order?

G: One Margaret pizza and one Napoli Pizza.

W: Anything to drink?

G: Coke, please.

W: No problem sir. Anything else? Would you like to try our new dish? It's super spicy buffalo wings and potato chips combo with sweet and sour sauce.

G: Sounds good. I would like a combo.

W: No problem, sir. May I have your name, phone number and the address so that we can deliver your order?

G: Sure. John Brown, 4569-9987. The address is No.34, West Madison Road.

W: Thank you, sir. We will get your order ready as soon as possible. Thanks for calling. Good bye.

Unit 10

中文翻譯

電話鈴聲響起……

W：午安您好，這裏是媽媽咪呀義式披薩店。請問我可以為您效勞嗎？

G：有的。我想要點外送，但我沒有在你們網站上看到菜單。

W：不好意思，先生。我們剛重新建立了我們的網站，請試看看這個連結：www.mamamiaitaliapizza.com.

G：好的，謝謝你。我待會在打。

五分鐘過後……

W：這裡是媽媽咪呀義式披薩店。請問我可以為您效勞嗎？

G：是的，我想要點外送餐。

W：好的，先生。請問想要點什麼口味的披薩呢？

G：一個瑪格麗特口味，一個拿破里口味。

W：想要喝點什麼嗎？

G：可樂，謝謝。

W：沒問題的，先生。還需要別的嗎？要不要嚐嚐我們的新菜色？超級麻辣水牛城雞翅及馬鈴薯片組合餐，搭配甜醋醬。

G：聽起來不錯，我要來一份。

W：不客氣，先生。請提供您的名字、電話號碼及地址，以方便我們替您送餐？

G：當然可以，John Brown，4569-9987。地址是梅迪森西街三十四號。

W：謝謝您，先生。我們將會備妥您的餐點，感謝您的來電，再見。

Unit 10

單字 Vocabulary

1. **sour** *adj.* 酸的
   例 I would like some sour candies before dinner.
   我喜歡在晚餐前來點酸的糖果。

2. **address** *n.* 地址
   例 I can't find his home address.
   我找不到他家的地址。

10.3 情境對話──和團體客導遊的應答
Dialogue with Tour Guides

Track 29

Waiter，服務生，簡稱 W。

Delivery Guy，外送員，簡稱 D。

Tour Guide, Mr. Brown 導遊，Brown 先生，簡稱 T。

W: Welcome to Happy Friday Restaurant. How may I help you?

T: Yes, I would like to order food delivery for ten sets of fried chicken combo.

W: No problem, sir. Anything to drink?

T: Coke, please.

W: We are promoting the super **spicy buffalo wings** now; you buy three sets then get one set for free. Would you like to try some?

T: No, thanks.

W: No problem, sir. By the way, may I have your name, phone number and the address so that we can deliver your order?

T: Sure. John Brown, 4569-9987. The address is No.34, West Madison Road. Wait, could you help to get the food delivered to the tour bus? I'm afraid by the time you arrive, we are about to set off soon. Sorry for the inconvenience it might cause.

W: Well, that will be no problem. Could you tell me the location where the bus stops?

T: It's the same address No. 34, West Madison Road. The bus will stop right in front of the hotel. I will be there waiting. If you have trouble finding us, just call me.

W: Ok. Got it, sir. Thanks for calling Good bye.

The delivery man arrives at No.34, West Madison Road and finds a tour bus stopped there. Now he needs to get the right person to have the food delivered. He is walking toward the tour bus and trying to ask a man standing there...

T: Oh, you are here. I'm John Brown. It's a relief you made it at the last moment.

D: Sorry about that. I'm stuck in the traffic on the way here. There you go with your food and the receipt.

T: Thank you.

Unit 10

中文翻譯

W：歡迎光臨快樂星期五餐廳，請問有可以幫忙的地方嗎

T：有的，我想要點外送餐點，十份炸雞組合餐。

W：沒問題，先生。請問要喝點什麼嗎？

T：可樂。

W：本店現在有促銷超級麻辣水牛城雞翅，買三組送一組，請問想要來一點試看看嗎？

T：不了，謝謝。

W：沒關係，先生。對了，請提供您的名字、電話號碼及地址，以方便我們替您送餐？

T：當然可以，John Brown，4569-9987。地址是梅迪森西街三十四號。等等，可以請您把外送送到巴士上嗎？我是擔心等你送到後，我們就要出發了。很抱歉為您帶來不便。

W：沒問題，可以告訴我巴士的位置嗎？

T：地址都是一樣的，梅迪森西街三十四號。巴士會停在飯店前，我會在那邊等，如果有任何問題，電話聯絡我就可以了。

W：好的，感謝來電，再見。

外送人員抵達梅迪森西街三十四號後，發現巴士就停在那。他需要找到人把外送送達，於是往巴士走去，正要問一問站在那的男士……

T：你晚到了，我是 John Brown，還好你在最後一刻趕到了。

D：很抱歉，我剛卡在路上了。這是您的外送和收據。

T：謝謝您。

單字 Vocabulary

1. **spicy** *adj.* 辣味的 水牛
   例 This Indian dish is too spicy. I can't bear it.
   這道印度菜太辣了，我受不了。

2. **buffalo** *n.* 水牛
   例 Buffaloes are the first things coming up to my mind when it comes to USA.
   一談到美國，我首先想到的是水牛。

3. **wing** *n.* 翅膀、羽翼
   例 The wings of this butterfly are broken.
   這蝴蝶的翅膀受傷了。

10.4 換句話說 In Other Words

May I have your name, phone number and the address so that we can deliver your order?

請提供您的名字、電話號碼及地址，以方便我們替您送餐？

☕ **For delivery, may I get your name, phone number and the address**?

為提供外送服務，我可以請您提供您的名字、電話號碼及地址嗎？

☕ **Could you provide me your information for food delivery**?

為了外送服務，可以請您提供您的資訊？

☕ **Please provide me your information for our delivery service.**

為了外送服務，可以請您提供您的資訊。

I would like to order food delivery.

我想點外送餐點。

☕ **Any food delivery available**?

有外送服務嗎？

☕ **May I have food delivery**?

我可以點外送服務嗎？

☕ **Do you provide the food delivery service**?

你有提供外送服務嗎？

I found there is a promotion of the premium business lunch set on the website now.

我看到網站上正在促銷豪華商業午餐。

I knew that you are promoting the premium business lunch set now.

我知道你們正在促銷豪華商業午餐。

I heard from my neighbor that the restaurant provides a discount for the premium business lunch set this month.

我從鄰居那得知餐廳這個月提供豪華商業午餐一個折扣。

The restaurant just released the news that for the first 100 customers, they are getting discount coupons for the premium signature food.

餐廳正發布消息，將給前 100 名顧客豪華招牌菜的高折扣優惠卷。

What kind of flavor would you like to have for your pizza?

請問想要點什麼口味的披薩呢？

Would you like to try the new flavor?

您想要試看看新口味嗎？

There are three new flavors you can choose. Would you like to try?

這裡有三種新口味可以給你做選擇。您想要試看看嗎？

What kind of flavor would you prefer?

哪種口味你比較喜歡呢？

Unit 11 外帶餐點
Takeout Service

11.1 情境對話──和商務客的應答
Dialogue with Business Customers

Track 30

*Waiter 服務生，簡稱 **W**。*

*Guest, Mr. Brown 商務客，Brown 先生，簡稱 **G**。*

The phone is ringing.

W: Good afternoon, this is Happy Friday Restaurant. How may I help you?

G: Yes. I would like to know if you have a takeout service.

W: Yes, sir. I can take an order for you.

G: Is the business set still available now?

W: Yes, business set is available for lunch and dinner.

G: Good. Then I would like to have ten sets, three **home-made** apple pies and seven honey lemon cakes.

W: No problem, sir. Would you like some appetizers?

G: What do you **recommend**?

W: Our best is **mashed** potato with blue cheese. Its portion is available for about five or six people. Would you like some?

G: Yes, we need two for that, please.

W: No problem, sir. When are you going to pick up your meal?

G: About 6:00 PM. Sorry, sir. I also need to get some drinks.

W: Ok. What would you like?

G: Two cups of coffee will do. Thank you.

W: Ok, sir. We will get your order ready then. Thanks for calling. See you at 6:00 PM. Good bye.

中文翻譯

電話鈴聲響起⋯⋯

W：午安您好，這裏是快樂星期五餐廳。請問我可以為您效勞嗎？

G：是的，我想知道你們有沒有提供外帶的服務？

W：有的，先生。我可以為您點餐。

G：請問現在還有提供商務餐嗎？

W：有的，我們的商務餐有提供午餐及晚餐。

G：太好了。那麼我想要十份商務餐，三個媽媽手作蘋果派及七個蜂蜜檸檬蛋糕。

W：沒問題，先生。請問你需要來點開胃菜嗎？

G：你推薦什麼呢？

W：我們賣最好的是馬鈴薯泥佐藍起司。份量大致可以五至六個人享用，您想要來一點嗎？

G：好的，來兩份，麻煩了。

W：沒問題，先生。請問您什麼時候要來取餐呢？

G：大概晚上六點。抱歉，我們還要點些飲料。

W：好的，請問想要喝什麼呢？

G：兩杯咖啡就可以了，謝謝。

W：好的，先生。我們將會備妥您的餐點，感謝您的來電，六點見囉，再見。

單字 Vocabulary

1. **home-made** *adj.* 自製的、家裡製的
   例 This is our home-made cake; please try some.
   這個是我們自製的蛋糕，請您品嚐。

2. **recommend** *v.* 推薦、建議
   例 The sales clerk recommends that I can buy the annual best-selling products for the birthday gift to my sister.
   銷售員推薦我購買年度熱銷產品來當作妹妹的生日禮物。

3. **mash** *v.* 把……搗碎、把……搗成糊狀
   例 Before baking the pumpkin pie, you have to mash the pumpkin with some flour.
   在烘烤南瓜派之前，你必須將南瓜與麵粉搗成糊狀。

11.2 情境對話——和家庭客的應答
Dialogue with Family Guests

 Track 31

*Waiter 服務生，簡稱 **W**。*

*Guest, Mr. Brown 家庭客，Brown 先生，簡稱 **G**。*

The phone is ringing.

W: Good afternoon, this is Mamamia Italian Pizzeria. How may I help you?

G: Yes. I would like to make a takeaway order, but I cannot find the menu on your website.

W: I'm sorry, sir. We just re-**established** our website. Please try this: www.mamamiaitaliapizza.com.

G: Ok, thank you. I'll call back later.

Five minutes later...

W: This is Mamamia Italian Pizzeria. How may I help you?

G: Yes, I would like to order a takeaway.

W: Ok, sir. What kind of **flavor** would you like to order?

G: One Margaret Pizza and one Napoli Pizza.

W: Anything to drink?

G: Any **carbonated** drinks?

W: Yes, sir. We only have 500ml of Pepsi, apple soda, and orange soda.

G: Two Pepsi, please.

W: No problem, sir. When would you like to pick up your order?

G: About 30 minutes later. Oh, do you take coupons? I have some from you last time.

W: Sorry, sir. The coupons are only available for guests coming to the restaurant.

G: Ok, I got it. I'm just asking. And we also want some ketchup and pepper, please.

W: Ok, we will get that ready too. Thanks for calling. See you then.

Unit 11

中文翻譯

電話鈴聲響起……

W：午安您好，這裡是媽媽咪呀義式披薩店。請問我可以為您效勞嗎？

G：有的。我想要點外帶，但我沒有在你們網站上看到菜單。

W：不好意思，先生。我們剛重新建立了我們的網站，請試看看這個連結：www.mamamiaitaliapizza.com.

G：好的，謝謝你。我待會在打。

五分鐘過後……

W：這裡是媽媽咪呀義式披薩店。請問我可以為您效勞嗎？

G：是的，我想要點外帶餐。

W：好的，先生。請問想要點什麼口味的披薩呢？

G：一個瑪格麗特口味，一個拿破里口味。

W：想要喝點什麼嗎？

G：有碳酸飲料嗎？

W：有的，先生。我們只有 500 毫升的百事可樂、蘋果蘇打及橘子蘇打。

G：兩個百事可樂，麻煩了。

W：不客氣，先生。請問您幾點要取餐呢？

G：大概三十分鐘後。喔對了，你們收折價券嗎？我上次從您拿了一些。

W：很抱歉，先生，折價券僅限來店用餐的顧客使用。

G：好的，我知道的，我只是問問。我們還要一些番茄醬和胡椒粉，麻煩您了。

W：好的，這些我們都會準備好，感謝您的來電，待會見囉！

Unit 11

單字 Vocabulary

1. **establish** *v.* 建立、創建
   例 It's hard to establish a commercial kingdom like that great businessman did.
   要像那位偉大的商人一樣創立商業王國是一件艱難的事。

2. **carbonated** *adj.* 含二氧化碳的、碳酸的
   例 Kids like to drink carbonated drinks like apple soda.
   孩子們喜歡喝碳酸飲料，如蘋果蘇打。

11.3 情境對話——和團體客導遊的應答
Dialogue with Tour Guides

🔘 *Track 32*

 Waiter，服務生，簡稱 W。

 Tour Guide, Mr. Brown 導遊，Brown 先生，簡稱 T。

W: Welcome to Happy Friday Restaurant. How may I help you?

T: Yes, I would like to order ten sets of fried chicken combo.

W: No problem, sir. Anything to drink?

T: Coke, please.

W: We are now **promoting** custard pie; you buy three then get one for free. Here is the **tryout**.

T: Thank you. It's delicious. I would like to have ten, please.

W: Sure, sir. I'm glad you like it. By the way, because it may take about 15 minutes for your order, would you like to be seated while waiting?

T: That's fine. I'll take my group members to walk around here and then come back to pick up the meals.

W: Ok, then see you later.

T: See you later. Wait. I forgot two of my group members are vegetarians so I have to order two vegetarian sets.

W: Sure. Two more vegetarian sets. Anything else, sir?

T: Well, get us some more ketchup and pepper. Thank you.

W: Ok. Here is the number for your takeout food. Remember to bring it with you for the food.

T: I will. Thank you.

Unit 11

中文翻譯

W：歡迎光臨快樂星期五餐廳，請問有可以幫忙的地方嗎？

T：有的，我想要點十份炸雞組合餐。

W：沒問題，先生。請問要喝點什麼嗎？

T：可樂。

W：本店現在有促銷卡士達派，買三送一，這是試吃品。

T：謝謝你，很好吃。我想要來十個，麻煩了。

W：沒問題，先生，我很開心你喜歡這個派。順帶一提，因為您的餐點需要約十五分鐘準備，請問您要不要稍坐等待？

T：不用了，我會和我的團員在這邊走走後，再回來拿餐點。

W：好的，那待會見囉。

T：那待會見。等等，我忘了我有兩個團員是吃素的，所以我要點兩份蔬食餐。

W：兩份蔬食餐，還需要些什麼嗎，先生？

T：我們還要一些番茄醬和胡椒粉。謝謝。

W：好的，這是您的外帶號碼，領取餐點時，別忘了一起帶來。

T：我會的，謝謝。

單字 Vocabulary

1. **promote** *v.* 促銷、推銷

   例 One of my jobs is to promote the new product.
   我的工作之一就是介紹新產品。

2. **tryout** *n.* 試用品、試吃

   例 Our company will organize a tryout in the beauty makeup exhibition.
   我們公司將會在美妝展覽會舉辦試用會。

11.4 換句話說 In Other Words

When would you like to pick up your meal?

您要什麼時候取餐呢？

What time would you like to pick up your order?

您要什麼時候取餐呢？

When would you prefer to take your order?

您想要什麼時候取餐呢？

What time will you pick up the meal?

您想要什麼時候取餐呢？

I would like to know if there is a takeout service?

我想知道你們有沒有提供外帶的服務？

Do you provide the takeout service?

你有提供外帶服務嗎？

Can I make a takeout order?

我能點外帶餐嗎？

Is the takeout service available now?

現在有外帶服務嗎？

Is the business set still available now?

請問現在還有提供商務餐嗎？

Can I order the business set now?

我可點商業餐嗎？

What time can I order the business set?

幾點開始可以點商務餐呢？

I would like to know if the business set still available now?

我想要知道哪時候可以點商務餐？

What do you recommend?

你推薦什麼呢？

Can you give us recommendations?

你推薦什麼呢？

What's the signature food?

招牌菜是什麼呢？

Can you offer us some suggestions?

你可以給個建議嗎？

Unit 12 吧檯服務 Bar Services

12.1 情境對話——和商務客的應答 Dialogue with Business Customers

 Track 33

*Bartender 酒保，簡稱 **B**。*

*Guest, Mr. Brown 商務客，Brown 先生，簡稱 **G**。*

Mr. Brown and his vendor, Jack are going to take some time off at a bar after finishing an all-day long meeting.

B: Hi. What would you like to drink?

G: Raspberry Coke and Lemon Lime Bitters, please.

B: Sure. I'll bring them to you soon.

G: Thanks!

Five minutes later, the bartender is back and gets Mr. Brown and his vendor Jack their drinks.

B: Here you are. Raspberry Coke and Lemon Lime Bitters. Enjoy!

G: Thanks! By the way, may I have more ice?

B: Sure, I'll get you some.

G: Thank you.

B: Here you are. I put them in a glass.

G: I would like to have some snacks. What kind of snacks do you provide?

B: We only have potato chips, crackers, and chocolate bars.

G: Potato chips, please.

B: Sure.

Unit 12

中文翻譯

在結束一整天的開會後，**Brown** 先生與他的廠商 **Jack** 正要去酒吧放鬆一下。

B：嗨，想喝點什麼嗎？

G：Raspberry Coke 及 Lemon Lime Bitters，麻煩了。

B：當然，我待會給您送過來。

G：謝謝！

五分鐘過後，酒保送飲料給 Brown 先生及他的廠商……

B：為您送上飲料，Raspberry Coke 及 Lemon Lime Bitters！請享用！

G：謝謝！對了，我可以要一些冰塊嗎？

B：當然可以，我等一下拿給您。

G：謝謝。

B：冰塊來了，我把它們裝在玻璃杯裡。

G：我想要再來些零食。你們有提供什麼零食？

B：我們只有馬鈴薯片、餅乾及巧克力條。

G：麻煩來些馬鈴薯片。

B：當然。

單字 Vocabulary

1. **vendor** *n.* 廠商、小販
   例 You can see there are lots of food vendors in the morning on the street.
   你可以在早上看到很多小吃攤販在這條路上。

2. **enjoy** *v.* 享受、享樂
   例 Mary really enjoys her vacation in Canada.
   Mary 真的很享受在加拿大的假期時光。

3. **chocolate** *n.* 巧克力
   例 I love the chocolate milk you bought for me.
   我喜歡你幫我買的巧克力牛奶。

4. **potato chips** *n.* 馬鈴薯片
   例 He has gained too much weight, so he quitted potato chips.
   他變胖了，只好戒掉馬鈴薯片。

Unit 12

12.2 情境對話——和家庭客的應答
Dialogue with Family Guests

 Track 34

*Bartender 酒保，簡稱 **B**。*

*Guest, Mr. Brown 家庭客，Brown 先生，簡稱 **G**。*

B: Hello, welcome to Happy Summer Lounge Bar. Is this your first time to our bar?

G: Yes, it's our first time. We're here to **celebrate** my mom's birthday. It has been a while since she went to a bar last time. So she told me she wants to have a special birthday party at the bar! And your bar is highly recommended by the waiter of the restaurant next door. That's why we are here.

B: Wow, that's really cool! By the way, do you need me to briefly introduce our menu to you?

G: Sure. Please go right ahead.

B: Our bar is suitable for families because we provide alcohol and non-alcohol drinks. There is a smoking area outside the front door; you can see this way if you have the need to smoke. **Basically**, smoking is **prohibited** in the **indoor** area.

G: I see.

B: Here is the menu. Please come to the bar counter to make an order.

G: Thank you.

B: You're welcome. Please take your time.

Five minutes later...

G: Hi, we would like to have three cocktails.

B: How about having some snacks to go with your cocktails?

G: Sounds good. What do you recommend?

B: Spiced Pickled Beets will be a good match with cocktails.

G: Ok, then we will have some of that as well. Thank you.

Unit 12

中文翻譯

B：哈囉，歡迎來到快樂夏季酒吧。您第一次來嗎？

G：是的，第一次來。我們來這裡慶祝我母親生日，她很久沒去過酒吧了，所以她告訴我很想在酒吧過生日。又剛好隔壁餐廳的服務生大力推薦你們這間酒吧，所以我們就來了。

B：哇噢，真的很酷！對了，容我簡單介紹一下我們酒吧嗎？

G：當然可以的，請說。

B：我們酒吧是家庭聚會也很適合的，所以我們提供酒精與非酒精飲料。若您有需要抽煙的話，從這裡可以看到，前門外面有個吸菸區。基本上，室內是禁止吸煙的。

G：我瞭解了。

B：這是菜單。請到吧檯櫃檯來點餐。

G：謝謝。

B：您別客氣，慢慢來。

（五分鐘後……）

G：您好，我們想要三杯雞尾酒。

B：那想要來些點心配雞尾酒嗎？

G：聽起來不錯，您推薦什麼呢？

B：辣醃甜菜不錯，很搭雞尾酒喔。

G：那就來一些吧，謝謝。

單字 Vocabulary

1. **celebrate** *v.* 慶祝、歡慶
   例 We're going to celebrate the opening anniversary of the shop.
   我們將要慶祝商店開幕一週年。

2. **basically** *adv.* 基本上
   例 Basically, we only have one week to prepare the party, so we have to hurry.
   基本上，我們只有一週的時間來準備宴會，所以我們必須加快腳步。

3. **prohibit** *v.* 禁止
   例 Talking loudly is prohibited during the concert.
   在音樂會演奏期間是禁止大聲說話的。

4. **indoor** *adj.* 室內的
   例 It's raining outside, so we can just stay in the indoor area.
   外面正在下雨，所以我們只能待在室內及等待。

Unit 12

12.3 情境對話——和團體客導遊的應答
Dialogue with Tour Guides

 Track 35

*Bartender 酒保，簡稱 **B**。*

*Tour Guide, Mr. Brown 導遊，Brown 先生，簡稱 **T**。*

B: Good evening. Welcome to Crazy Jungle Bar. How are you?

T: We're all good, thank you.

B: Is this your first time here?

T: Yes. We're from New York.

B: Wow. Welcome! So, do you need me to briefly introduce what we have on our menu to you?

T: Sure, please go right ahead.

B: Here is the menu. Our main beverage are cocktails. There are different cocktails on this **page** and the next page for your choices. Or if you want some beer, please **turn** to page four. If you don't want alcohol, we do have non**alcoholic** beverage as you see on the last page.

T: I see.

B: If you want some snacks to go with your drinks, please turn to the last page. And come to the bar counter to make your order. I'll be there for you.

T: Is smoking **permitted** here?

B: Yes.

T: Ok. Thank you.

B: You're welcome, sir.

Three minutes later...

T: We'd like to have one Spicy Spaghetti, two Creamed Mashed Potatoes and three Long Island Iced Tea.

B: Sure. Here are your water while you are waiting for your meal.

中文翻譯

B：晚安您好，歡迎來到瘋狂叢林酒吧。你們好嗎？

T：我們都很好，謝謝。

B：第一次來嗎？

T：是的，我們來自紐約。

B：哇噢，真的很歡迎您們。那麼，容我簡單介紹一下本酒吧嗎？

T：當然好的，請說。

B：這是菜單。我們主要提供的飲料為調酒，在本頁及下一頁有不同的調酒供您選擇。或是你想來點啤酒，請翻到第四頁。即使您不想要喝酒，我們也有提供無酒精飲料，在最後一頁。

T：我瞭解了。

B：如果您想要些點心配飲料，請翻到菜單的最後一頁。接著，請到酒吧櫃檯，我將會在那為您服務。

T：這裡可以吸菸嗎？

B：可以的。

T：好的，謝謝。

B：您別客氣，先生。

三分鐘後……

T：我們想要一份辣味義大利麵、兩份奶油馬鈴薯泥和三杯長島冰茶。

B：好的，在餐點來之前，這是給您的水。

單字 Vocabulary

1. **permit** *v.* 允許
   例 Driving is not permitted after having alcohol.
   喝酒後開車是不被允許的。

2. **alcoholic** *adj.* 酒精的
   例 We offer alcoholic and nonalcoholic drinks.
   我們有提供酒精與非酒精類的飲品。

3. **page** *n.* 頁面
   例 The information you need is on the main page of this website.
   您要的資訊放在網頁的主要頁面上。

4. **turn** *v.* 翻；轉彎
   例 He bumped into his ex-girlfriend when he turned right on this corner.
   他在轉角右轉後，撞見他的前女友。

12.4 換句話說 In Other Words

What would you like to drink?

想要喝點什麼嗎？

🍵 **What kind of beverage do you prefer**?

您想喝點什麼？

🍵 **Which beverage would you like to order**?

您想點什麼來喝呢？

🍵 **What would you like for beverage**?

您想喝點什麼？

Do you need me to briefly introduce what we have on our menu to you?

容我簡單介紹一下本酒吧嗎？

🍵 **May I show you our bar**?

可以容我簡單介紹一下本酒吧嗎？

🍵 **Would you like me to briefly introduce the bar for you**?

您需要我簡單介紹一下酒吧嗎？

🍵 **Would you like to know more about our bar**?

您需要我簡單認識一下酒吧嗎？

I would like to have some snacks.

我想要再來些零食。

🥤 **I want to have more snacks.**

我想多吃點零食。

🥤 **Would you give me more snacks?**

可以給我多一點零食嗎？

🥤 **May I have another snacks or sweets?**

我可以要其他的零食或甜食嗎？

What kind of snacks do you provide?

你們有提供什麼零食？

🥤 **Do you provide the Italian snacks?**

你有提供義式口味的零嘴嗎？

🥤 **What kind of snacks can I have?**

我可以要哪種零食呢？

🥤 **Is there any snacks provided for vegetarians?**

有提供給蔬食者的零嘴嗎？

Unit 12

Unit 13 自助餐服務 Buffet Services

13.1 情境對話──和商務客的應答 Dialogue with Business Customers

 Track 36

 *Waiter 服務生，簡稱 **W**。*

 *Guest, Mr. Brown 商務客，Brown 先生，簡稱 **G**。*

W: Hello, welcome to Happy Friday Restaurant. How may I help you?

G: Yes. I need a table for ten people.

W: Sure, we have a table available for ten people, sir. Please notice that we only offer buffet service today.

G: That's ok. We know that.

W: Ok, This way please. Here is your table. May I briefly introduce what we have for the buffet service to you?

G: Sure.

W: Our restaurant is famous for **various foreign** cuisines. We have **Dim Sum** in area A, Italian in area B, French in area C, and Indian cuisines in area D. Today is the buffet service day, so you can try all of those cuisines for $75 per person.

G: Excuse me. My company is the premium member of the restaurant. Is there any discount for the premium member?

W: Yes, sir. Premium member will get 10% off of the original charge.

G: Ok.

W: Please notice that the **flatware** is on the counter at the corner.

G: Thank you.

W: Then you could start to pick up your meal now. Enjoy!

中文翻譯

W：哈囉，歡迎光臨快樂星期五餐廳。請問我能幫您什麼忙嗎？

G：是的，我需要十人的位置。

W：當然好的，我們有十人座的位置，先生。煩請您留意一下，今天我們只提供自助餐的服務。

G: 沒關係。

W：好的，這邊請。這是您的位置。請問我可以為您簡單介紹一下餐廳自助餐的服務嗎？

G：當然可以。

W：本餐廳最有名的是異國料理，我們A區有港式料理、B區有義式料理、C區有法式料理及D區是印度料理。今天是自助餐日，您可以以每人 75 元的價格享用所有的料理。

G：不好意思，請問我的公司是你們的特級會員，請問有任何折扣嗎？

W：有的，先生。特等貴賓享有原價九折優惠。

G：好的。

W：請留意，餐具在轉角的那個櫃檯上。

G：謝謝你。

W：那麼您現在可以開始取餐了，請慢用。

單字 Vocabulary

1. **various** *adj.* 不同的、種類多的
   例 There are various services provided by this company.
   這間公司提供許多種服務。

2. **foreign** *adj.* 外國的
   例 Mary wants to learn a foreign language.
   瑪麗想要學外語。

3. **Dim Sum** *n.* 廣式點心
   例 The desserts in Hong Kong are commonly called Dim Sum pronounced in Cantonese.
   香港的點心泛稱點心（粵語發音）。

4. **flatware** *n.* 餐具
   例 Flatware includes knives, forks and spoons.
   餐具包含刀叉及湯匙。

13.2 情境對話——和家庭客的應答
Dialogue with Family Guests

 Track 37

Waiter 服務生，簡稱 W。

Guest, Mr. Brown 家庭客，Brown 先生，簡稱 G。

W: Hello, welcome to Happy Friday Restaurant. How may I help you?

G: Yes, I would like a table for four.

W: Ok, please follow me in this way.

The waiter leads the Brown family to their table.

W: Sir and madam, may I briefly introduce what we have for the buffet service to you?

G: Sure.

W: Today is European **buffet** day. All the meals served are Italian, French and Spanish cuisines. Italian cuisine is in Area A, French cuisine is in Area B and Spanish cuisine is in Area C. We also **prepare** specialties for the kids if they don't like the cuisines mentioned earlier. If you have any needs for your children, please let us know.

G: Sounds great. Thank you for the introduction. By the way, we have some coupons with us. Can we have a discount with those coupons?

W: Sorry, sir. These coupons are not available on the European buffet day.

G: Ok, thank you. I'm just asking.

W: It's fine. And you could start to pick up your meal now. Everything you need, including silverware and sauces, is over there. Enjoy!

G: We will. Thank you.

W: You are welcome, sir.

Two and half hours later...

W: Sir and madam. Here to remind you that you still have twenty minutes left for the buffet service.

G: Thank you. We will mind the time.

Unit 13

中文翻譯

W：哈囉，歡迎光臨快樂星期五餐廳。請問我能幫您什麼忙嗎？

G：是的，我想要一張四人的座位。

W：好的，這邊請跟我來。

服務生帶領 Brown 一家人到他們的位置……

W：先生及女士，請問我可以簡單為您介紹本餐廳自助餐的服務嗎？

G：當然可以。

W：今天是歐式自助餐日，所有提供的餐點皆為義式、法式及西班牙風味美食。義式料理位於 A 區、法式料理位於 B 區及西班牙風味美食在 C 區。若小朋友不喜歡剛剛前述的料理，我們也有為小朋友提供替別的餐點。若您的小朋友有需要，請讓我們知道。

G：當然好的。

W：那麼您現在可以開始取餐了，請慢用。

G：聽起來真不錯，謝謝您的介紹，對了我們還有些折價券，請問可以用嗎？

W：很抱歉，先生。折價券不能用在歐洲自助餐日喔。

G：我了解了，謝謝您，我只是問問。

W：沒關係的，您現在可以取餐了。任何您需要的，包括餐具和醬料，都在那了，祝您用餐愉快。

G：好的，謝謝您。

W：您別客氣，先生。

兩個半小時後……

W：您好，在此提醒您還有 20 分鐘享用自助餐服務。

G：謝謝您，我們會注意時間。

單字 Vocabulary

1. **buffet** *n.* 自助餐
   例 This buffet restaurant is so popular that you won't have a table if you don't make a reservation in advance.
   這間自助餐廳很有名，你若沒有預先訂位就吃不到了。

2. **prepare** *v.* 準備
   例 Ted didn't prepare for his exam, so he didn't get a good result.
   泰德沒有為他的考試作準備，所以他考差了。

13.3 情境對話——和團體客導遊的應答
Dialogue with Tour Guides

 Track 38

 Waiter 服務生，簡稱 W。

 Tour Guide, Amy 導遊，Amy 小姐，簡稱 T。

W: Hello, welcome to Happy Friday Restaurant. How may I help you?

T: Hi, I'm Amy, the tourist of Asia Tour. I've made a reservation this morning.

W: Hello, Miss Amy. Let's me check it for you. Please wait. Yes, miss. Please follow me this way.

T: Ok.

W: This is the private room for your group. Is there a need for me to introduce our restaurant service for you?

T: Yes, please.

W: We provide buffet service today, and all the meals served are available for one price only. You could have Italian **cuisine** in Area A, Japanese cuisine in Area B and Chinese cuisine in

Area C. It's all free of charge for any nonalcoholic beverages, and the charge of the alcoholic beverages depends on the **type** you order. If you need the menu for alcoholic beverages, please let us know.

T: Ok. Do you have the time limitation for the buffet service?

W: Thank you for asking. Yes, we do. The buffet service is from 1:30 to 4:30.

T: Ok, I got it. Thank you.

W: You're welcome, madam. Then you could start to pick up your meal now. Everything you need, including napkins, sauces and silverware, is over there. Enjoy!

Later...

T: Excuse, there are no more napkins on the counter. Could you please bring us some more new napkins?

W: Sure.

T: And some of plates in the Area A are empty. Please get them refilled.

W: Sure. Thank you for reminding us.

中文翻譯

W：哈囉，歡迎光臨快樂星期五餐廳。請問我能幫您什麼忙嗎？

T：嗨，我是亞洲之行的導遊 Amy。我今天早上有預約。

W：哈囉，Amy 小姐。請稍等，我為您查一下。是的，小姐。請跟我來。

T：好的。

W：這是您的團體包廂。請問需要由我來為您及貴賓們介紹一下本餐廳服務嗎？

T：好的，麻煩了。

W：我們今天提供自助餐服務，只需單一價就可以享用所有的美食。您可以在 A 區選用義式美食、在 B 區選用日式料理及 C 區為中式料理。任何非酒精飲料都是免費的，但酒精性飲料依種類計費。若您需要酒精性飲料的菜單，請讓我們知道。

T：好的。請問您的自助餐服務有時間限制嗎？

W：謝謝您的詢問，是的，我們有限制，自助餐服務時間是 1:30 到 4:30。

T：好的，我了解了。謝謝您。

W：別客氣。您可以取餐了，所有您需要的，包括餐巾、醬料和餐具都在那了，祝您用餐愉快。

稍後……

T：不好意思，櫃台上已沒有餐巾了，可以請您補新的餐巾嗎？

W：沒問題。

T：A 區的一些餐盤空了，也麻煩幫忙補一下。

W：好的，感謝您特地提醒。

單字 Vocabulary

1. **cuisine** *n.* 美食

   例 We like to taste different foreign cuisine abroad.
   我們喜歡出國品嚐不同的異國美食。

2. **type** *n.* 種類、類型

   例 Mary told me that John is not the type of boys she likes.
   瑪麗告訴我，約翰不是她喜歡的類型。

May I briefly introduce what we have for the buffet service for you?

請問我可以簡單介紹一下本餐廳自助餐的服務嗎？

☕ **May I briefly introduce our service to you**?

請問能容我簡短介紹一下我們的服務給您嗎？

☕ **May I show you the services that we provide**?

請問能容我簡短介紹一下我們的服務給您嗎？

☕ **Would you mind if I briefly show you the services provided by our restaurant**?

請問能容我簡短介紹一下我們的服務給您嗎？

Please notice that we only offer buffet service today.

煩請您留意一下，今天我們只提供自助餐的服務。

☕ **Only buffet service is provided. Please kindly notice that.**

這裡只有提供自助餐服務。請諒解。

☕ **I'm afraid that we just provide the buffet service today.**

我很抱歉我們今天只提供自助餐服務。

☕ **Is it ok for you that there is only buffet service provided today**?

今天只提供自助餐服務，這樣您可以嗎？

Is there any discount for the premium member?

請問會員有任何折扣嗎？

Any discount for the club member?

會員有任何折扣嗎？

I'm the club member. Can I have a discount?

我是會員。可以有折扣嗎？

May I use the coupon for this service?

這個服務可以使用這個折價券嗎？

If you have any needs for your children, please let us know.

若您的小朋友有需要，請讓我們知道。

We offer the kid's meal as well. Please let me know if you need one.

我們提供兒童餐。若您有需要請讓我知道。

Kid's meal is available for now. Would you like to order one for the kid?

兒童餐現在可以點囉。您有要為您的小孩點一份嗎？

Please let me know if you have any needs for the infant.

若您有需要任何給小嬰孩的服務，請讓我知道。

職場補給站 Must-Know Tips

　　你知道，隨著時代的進步，支付工具（payment instrument）也是很多元的嗎？通常來說，支付方式有現金付款（cash）、轉帳付款（transfer）、匯款付款（remittance）及信用卡付款（credit card）等等。還有一種付款方式，很類似信用卡付款，也是使用刷卡的方式，但扣款方式大大不相同，你知道是什麼嗎？答案就是轉帳卡（debit card）或稱借記卡，在美國則稱為支票卡（check card），它是一種扣款方式，在消費的時候，直接在商店刷卡，透過銀行存款扣款，所以銀行存款有多少錢，就扣多少錢，因此不會產生超刷（over limit）、透支（bank overdraft）及產生循環利息（interest）等問題。

☆ 匯帳（remittance）：

付款方須親自到銀行或郵局，填寫匯款單，交付現金給行員；而在收款方，只會看得到付款方的姓名，不會有其他銀行資訊。

☆ 轉帳（transfer）：

透過自動櫃員機（Automatic Teller Machine, ATM），將款項由A帳戶轉到B帳戶的一種方式。此種方式可以清楚知道款項的轉出與轉入，是一種很方便的付款方式。

重要句型整理 Useful Sentences

① **May I get your name and phone number?**
請您給我您的姓名與電話號碼。

② **Your booking cancellation is completed.**
您的訂位已完成取消。

③ **Would you like to be seated while waiting?**
那您要坐著等嗎？

④ **Please mind your step.**
請小心台階。

⑤ **Have you got the reservation?**
請問您有訂位嗎？

⑥ **Would you come with me, please?**
可以請您跟我來嗎？

⑦ **Would you like smoking or non-smoking area?**
您想要吸煙區或非吸煙區呢？

⑧ **I'll be your server this evening.**
今晚由我為您服務。

⑨ **I'll be back with your order shortly.**
我稍等將餐點送過來給您。

⑩ **How would you like your stakes?**
您想要牛排幾分熟呢？

Unit
01 會議
Meetings

1.1 情境對話——和商務客的應答 1
Dialogue with Business Customers 1

 Track 39

Receptionist 櫃台人員，簡稱 **R**。

Guest, Mr. Brown 商務客，*Brown* 先生，簡稱 **G**。

The telephone is ringing...

R: Good afternoon, this is Happy Friday Restaurant. How may I help you?

G: Yes, I would like to make a reservation for a conference room. Could you briefly introduce the **conference** room or the related services for me?

R: Sure, sir. There are three types of conference rooms that we provide: the **maximum** capacity of a small conference room is 5 people; a medium conference room is 15 people and a large conference room is 30 people. All types of conference rooms are equipped with modern **audiovisual** equipment, including projectors for computers, **slides** and films. Each conference room has an indoor coffee break area as well.

G: That's good. We also need the lunch included.

R: Certainly, sir. We can arrange the lunch for you; the restaurant provides the business lunch, especially for the conference guests.

G: Good. Could you please send me a menu so that I can decide the meal and the related quotations, including the conference charge and meal charge?

R: No problem, sir. Your email address, please?

G: danielbrown@jscor.com

R: Ok, I will send the related information to you very soon.

中文翻譯

電話鈴聲響起……

R：午安您好，這裡是快樂星期五餐廳。請問有什麼需要嗎？

G：是的，我想要預約會議室。可以請你為我簡單介紹一下會議室或相關服務嗎？

R：當然沒問題的，先生。本餐廳提供三種會議中心，小型會議室最多可容納五人、中型會議室最多可容納十五人及大型會議室最多可容納三十人。所有類型的會議室皆配有最新視聽配備、投影機可用於電腦、投影片及影片，以及室內的休息餐區。

G：那很不錯，我們也需要包含午餐。

R：當然囉，先生。我們可以為您安排午餐的部分，我們有特別提供參與會議貴賓的商務午餐。

G：很好。麻煩你寄個菜單給我，讓我可以決定要選什麼餐點，以及包含會議費用及餐費的相關報價單。

R：沒問題，先生。請提供您的電子郵件地址。

G：danielbrown@jscor.com

R：好的，我將會很快地寄給您相關訊息。

單字 Vocabulary

1. **conference** *n.* 會議

   例 Don't bother the manager while he's speaking in the conference.

   經理在會議談話，請不要打擾他。。

2. **maximum** *adj.* 最大、最多

   例 The maximum capacity of the elevator is20 people.

   這台電梯最多乘載 20 人。

3. **audiovisual** *adj.* 視聽

   例 Thanks to the modern technology, We have a lot of audiovisual equipment for us to choice from.

   拜近代科技所賜，我們有許多視聽設備可供選擇。

4. **slide** *n.* 投影片

   例 Slides can help elaborate the presentation better during the meeting.

   投影片在開會時可以提供更好的解說。

1.2 情境對話──和商務客的應答 2
Dialogue with Business Customers 2

 Track 40

Receptionist 櫃台人員，簡稱 **R**。

Guest, Mr. Brown 商務客，*Brown* 先生，簡稱 **G**。

The telephone is ringing...

R: Good morning, this is Happy Friday Restaurant. How may I help you?

G: Yes, this is Mr. Brown. I would like to make a reservation for a conference room.

R: Hello, Mr. Brown. It's great to hear from you again. When would you prefer for the conference room?

G: Next Friday. Is it still available?

R: Yes, sir. How many people will there be in your party?

G: 17.

R: Then I suggest that you book the large conference room for your request.

G: OK.

R: And how about the lunch?

G: I prefer to have plan B.

R: No problem, sir.

G: I will e-mail you the details and the schedule of our meeting. And please arrange the coffee break meals and beverages.

R: No problem, sir.

G: Thanks. By the way, when is the **deadline** to pay the deposit?

R: This Friday is the last day to pay the deposit, sir. How would you like to pay the deposit?

G: I will make a transfer. Could you give me the bank account of the restaurant?

R: Please kindly notice that there is a bank account shown on the **quotation** that was sent to you yesterday.

Unit 01

中文翻譯

電話鈴聲響起……

R：早安您好，這裡是快樂星期五餐廳。請問有什麼需要嗎？

G：是的，我是 Brown 先生。我想要預訂一間會議室。

R：哈囉，Brown 先生。很開心又再次與您通話。您想要訂什麼時候的
會議室呢？

G：下週五，請問還能訂嗎？

R：可以的，先生。請問有幾位要參與的呢？

G：十七位。

R：那麼我建議您預定大間的會議室，以符合您人數的需求。

G：好的。

R：那午餐呢？

G：我要 B 計畫。

R：沒問題，先生。

G：我將會寄份有關我們會議的細節及時程表給你。請幫我安排休息時間
的餐點及飲料。

R：沒問題，先生。

G：謝了。對了，訂金最晚哪一天要支付呢？

R：本週五是最後一天支付訂金，先生。請問您要用怎樣的支付方式呢？

G：我會使用轉帳方式。麻煩提供貴餐廳的銀行帳戶。

R：請您留意一下昨天寄給您的報價單上有顯示我們飯店的銀行帳戶。

單字 Vocabulary

1. **deadline** *n.* 期限、限期

   例 The manager asked his staff to finish the project before the deadline.

   經理要求他的下屬在期限前完成案件。

2. **quotation** *n.* 報價、行情

   例 My boss didn't accept the quotation that our vendor provided last Friday.

   我老闆不接受上禮拜五廠商提供的報價。

1.3 情境對話——和商務客的應答 3
Dialogue with Business Customers 3

 Track 41

 Receptionist 櫃台人員，簡稱 R。

 Guest, Mr. Brown 商務客，Brown 先生，簡稱 G。

Before the meeting starts...

R: Good morning, Mr. Brown.

G: Good morning. Is everything all well prepared?

R: Don't worry, sir. Everything is all well prepared. And the equipment will be checked twice before the conference starts.

G: Good.

R: We will send three waiters to **assist** the conference if there is anything that needs to be **solved** immediately. The coffee break meals and beverages will be in the coffee break area right on the left side of the conference room door.

G: Thanks!

R: You're welcome, sir. If there is any question or service that needs to be solved and provided, please let me know.

G: I will.

Checking the bill...

R: Hello Mr. Brown. How was the meeting? Was everything all right?

G: Yes, the meeting went well. Thanks!

R: You're welcome, sir. Here is the invoice. It's $5,500 after **deducting** the deposit you have **prepaid** and 10% tax is included. How would you like to pay the bill?

G: Credit card, please.

R: No problem. Your credit card, please.

Unit 01

中文翻譯

在會議開始之前……

R：早安，Brown 先生。

G：早安。一切都準備好了吧？

R：您放心，先生。一切準備就緒，所有的設備在開始前會再次檢查。

G：很好。

R：我們將會指派三位服務生來提供會議的協助，若有任何需要，可以立即提供及處理。休息時間用的餐點及飲料將會在休息區準備妥當，休息區就在會議室門口的左手邊。

G：謝謝！

R：您別客氣，先生。若有任何問題或需要提供的服務，請讓我知道。

結帳中……

R：哈囉，Brown 先生。會議進行如何？一切都還好嗎？

G：是的，會議很順利。謝謝！

R：您別客氣，先生。這是您的發票。再扣掉您先前預付的訂金後，應付
金額為 5,500 元，含 10% 稅。請問您要用什麼付款方式？

G：信用卡。

R：沒問題，請提供您的信用卡。

單字 Vocabulary

1. **assist** *v.* 協助、幫助
   例 I'll assist the remaining process of the research.
   我將會協助剩餘的研究過程。

2. **solve** *v.* 解決
   例 The thorny issue s have been solved finally.
   這些棘手問題終於被解決了。

3. **deduct** *v.* 扣除
   例 The penalty fee will be deducted from your pay diretly.
   罰款會直接從您的薪水扣除。

4. **prepaid** *adj.* 預付的、預先支付的
   例 The store manager asked the customer to make a prepaid
   payment half the original price.
   店經理要求顧客預先支付半數款項。

1.4 換句話說 In Other Words

When would you prefer for the conference room?
請問您要預訂什麼時間的會議室？

☕ **What time would you like to book for the conference room?**
請問您要預訂什麼時間的會議室？

☕ **What time would you like to reserve the conference room?**
請問您要預訂什麼時間的會議室？

☕ **What time would you like for your conference room reservation?**
請問您要預訂什麼時間的會議室？

Could you briefly introduce the conference room or the related services for me?
可以請你為我簡單介紹一下會議室或相關服務嗎

☕ **Could you introduce the utilities in the conference room?**
可以介紹一下會議室的設施嗎？

☕ **I would like to know the conference service and the utilities you may provide.**
我想要知道會議室服務及相關設施的提供服務。

☕ **May I ask about the conference room service?**
我可以詢問會議室服務嗎？

We also need the lunch included.

我們也需要包含午餐。

Any food and beverage services are included in the conference room service?

酒水服務有包含在會議室服務裡嗎？

Do we need to order the lunch additionally?

我們需要額外預定午餐嗎？

Does the conference room service include the food and beverage service?

會議室服務有包含酒水服務嗎？

Please let me know if you decide to make a reservation.

若您要預訂的話，請讓我知道。

Please give me a call if you need to make a reservation

若您要預訂，請電話聯繫我。

Please remind me if you would like to make the reservation.

如果您有意願要預訂，請提醒我。

If you want to book with a fair price, please let me know in advance.

若您想要預訂一個好的折扣，請事先讓我知道。

Unit 02　婚宴　Weddings

2.1 情境對話——和家庭客的應答 1
Dialogue with Business Family Guests 1

 Track 42

*Receptionist 櫃台人員，簡稱 **R**。*

*Guest, Mr. Brown 家庭客，Brown 先生，簡稱 **G**。*

The telephone is ringing...

R: Good afternoon, this is Happy Friday Restaurant. How may I help you?

G: Yes, I would like to know if there is any service provided for the wedding party?

R: Yes, we have a great location for wedding ceremony.

G: Good. Could you briefly introduce me the environment and related equipment you have for a wedding?

R: No problem, sir. Our restaurant can accommodate up to 400 people and is an ideal place for private or institutional events, and romantic dinners as well. We also have modern audiovisual equipment as well as stages and lighting for the ceremony purposes.

G: Sounds good. I would like to have the service quotation to make the decision.

R: Sure, we can provide the service quotation to you for your requirement. How may I reach you?

G: It's better to fax the information to me. Here is my fax number 786-5544.

R: Ok, I will send the related information to you very soon.

G: Thank you.

R: You're welcome, sir. Please let me know if you decide to make a reservation. Have a nice day!

Unit 02

中文翻譯

電話鈴聲響起……

R：午安您好，這裡是快樂星期五餐廳。請問有我可以提供您服務的地方嗎？

G：是的，我想要知道貴餐廳有沒有提供婚宴服務？

R：有的，我們有提供很棒的婚禮場地。

G：很好。那麻煩請你為我簡單介紹場地環境及相關設備好嗎？

R：沒問題的，先生。我們餐廳最多可容納 400 人，是個最適合私人及機構團體聚會的場所，若作為浪漫晚餐的場所也非常適合。我們也配備了最新穎的視聽設備、舞台及燈光設備，可符合婚禮儀式的需求。

G：聽起來不錯。我想要服務的報價好做出決定。

R：當然沒問題，我們提供服務報價給您參考。請問怎麼提供給您服務報價呢？

G：最好是將資料傳真給我。這是我的傳真號碼 786-5544。

R：好的，我將盡快將訊息傳真給您。

G：謝謝你。

R：您別客氣，先生。若有需要訂位，再煩請讓我知道。祝您有美好的一
天。

單字 Vocabulary

1. **ceremony** *n.* 典禮、儀式

   例 The wedding ceremony will be held on January 15.
   結婚典禮將會在一月十五號舉行。

2. **environment** *n.* 環境

   例 The Brown family moved to Berlin for a better educational
   environment for their children.
   布朗一家為了給孩子更好的教育環境而搬到柏林去。

3. **accommodate** *v.* 容納

   例 This banquet room can accommodate up to 300 guests.
   宴會廳最多可容納 300 名的賓客。

註：其它單字請見 2.2。

2.2 情境對話——和家庭客的應答 2
Dialogue with Family Guests 2

 Track 43

 Receptionist 櫃台人員，簡稱 R。

 Guest, Mr. Brown 家庭客，Brown 先生，簡稱 G。

The telephone is ringing...

R: Good morning, this is Happy Friday Restaurant. How may I help you?

G: Yes, this is Mr. Brown. I would like to make a reservation for a wedding party.

R: Hello, Mr. Brown. It's great to hear from you again. When would you prefer for the wedding party?

G: November 12. I plan to have an opening with a cocktails party at 10:30 in the morning and then lunch service at 12:30 PM.

R: No problem, sir. Have you decided the plan of meal to be served?

G: Yes, I chose the Romantic French Garden Buffet Plan.

R: Sir, this type is for outdoor service. If you would like to have indoor services, you need to choose another plan.

G: I think outdoor service is good.

R: Ok. How many people will attend the party?

G: Approximately 50 people.

R: Ok. Anything else we can do for you?

G: Yes, I would like to have white and red roses to decorate the wedding space.

R: No problem, sir.

中文翻譯

電話鈴聲響起……

R：早安您好，這裡是快樂星期五餐廳。請問有我可以提您服務的地方
嗎？

G：是的，我是 Brown 先生。我想要預訂婚宴派對。

R：哈囉，Brown 先生。很開心再次聽到您的來電。您想要預定哪個時
間的生日派對呢？

G：十一月十二號。我計劃當天早上十點半來個雞尾酒會當作開幕，然後
中午十二點半開始午餐。

R：沒問題的，先生。您有決定好要選那個餐點服務計畫了嗎？

G：有的，我選浪漫法式花園自助餐計畫。

R：先生，這個計畫是戶外的服務喔。若您想要選擇室內服務的話，請選
別的計畫喔。

G：我覺得室外不錯。

R：好的。請問有幾位來賓要參加派對呢？

G：大約 50 人。

R：好的，請問還有別的需要嗎？

G：有的，我想要用白玫瑰與紅玫瑰來裝飾婚禮場地。

R：沒問題的，先生。

單字 Vocabulary

1. **institutional** *adj.* 公共團體的、制度的
   例 This gathering is for institutional changes of the company.
   這個聚會是為了公司要改變制度而舉辦。

2. **fax** *v.* 傳真
   例 Please fax this to the vendor before this afternoon.
   請在下午前將這個傳真給廠商。

2.3 情境對話──和家庭客的應答 3
Dialogue with Family Guests 3

 Track 44

Receptionist 櫃台人員，簡稱 **R**。

Guest, Mr. Brown 家庭客，*Brown* 先生，簡稱 **G**。

Before the cocktails party starts...

R: Good morning, Mr. Brown.

G: Good morning. Is everything all well prepared?

R: Don't worry, sir. Everything is all well prepared.

G: Good.

R: The cocktail party will start on time, and we will send three waiters to assist the party and double check the equipment as well.

G: Thank you.

R: You're welcome, sir. If there is any request to be served, please kindly let me know. Have a great time.

Checking the bill...

R: Hi, Mr. Brown. How was the wedding? Was everything going well?

G: Yes, the wedding party was perfect. Both my guests and we had a great time. Thanks for the assistance that you all provided today.

R: You're welcome, sir. We're glad you had a great time. Would you like to pay now?

G: Yes, please.

R: Ok. Here is the invoice for you. The remaining service fee after deducting the deposit you have prepaid earlier is $1,880 including the 10% sales tax. How would you like to make your payment?

G: Credit card, please.

R: Ok. Thank you for choosing our restaurant.

Unit 02

中文翻譯

雞尾酒會開始前……

R：早安，Brown 先生。

G：早安，一切都準備好了嗎？

R：別擔心，先生。一切都已就緒。

G：很好。

R：雞尾酒會將準時開始，我們將會派三位服務生來協助派對之進行，以及再度確認設備狀態。

G：謝謝你。

R：您別客氣，先生。若有其他需要服務的地方，請您讓我知道。祝您有美好的一天。

結帳中……

R：嗨，Brown 先生。婚禮還好嗎？一切都還順利嗎？

G：是的，婚禮非常的完美。我的賓客及我們夫婦倆都玩得很愉快。感謝你們今天提供的協助。

R：您別客氣，先生。我們替您感到開心。請問您要結帳了嗎？

G：是的，麻煩了。

R：好的，這是您的發票。扣掉您的訂金後，剩下應付服務費用為 1,880 元含 10% 銷售稅。您要怎麼支付呢？

G：信用卡。

R：好的。感謝您選擇本飯店。

Unit 02

單字 Vocabulary

1. **perfect** *adj.* 完美的、無暇的
   例 I have a perfect girlfriend.
   我有個完美女友。

2. **assistance** *n.* 協助、幫助
   例 I really appreciate your assistance yesterday.
   我真的很感謝你昨天的協助。

2.4 換句話說 In Other Words

How would you like to pay the deposit?

您想用什麼方式支付訂金呢？

How would you like the deposit to be paid?

您想用什麼方式支付訂金呢？

Would you to pay the deposit by cash or by credit card?

您想用什麼方式支付訂金呢？現金或信用卡？

What kind of payment would you choose for prepaying the deposit?

您想用什麼方式支付訂金呢？

We have a great location for wedding ceremony.

我們有提供很棒的婚禮場地。

There are two great locations for the wedding.

我們有兩個很棒的場地提供給婚禮用途。

We have a beautiful church for your wedding.

我們有一座很漂亮的教堂，可以滿足你婚禮上的需要。

We provide a church as a wedding location for our customers.

我們提供一座教堂給客人舉辦婚禮。

Have you decided meal plan to be served?

您有決定好要選那個餐點服務計畫了嗎？

Which service plan will you choose?

你會想哪個服務方案？

Would you like to choose the plan A?

您想要選方案 **A** 嗎？

Do you consider the plan A? It's really good for you.

你有考慮方案 **A** 嗎？這很適合你。

How many people will attend the party?

請問有幾位來賓要參加派對呢？

How many guests would you like to invite?

您想要邀請幾位來賓呢？

How many people are going to attend the party?

有多少人將要參加這個派對呢？

The party is available for almost 100 people. Is it ok?

這個派對可容納差不多 100 人。這樣可以嗎？

Unit
03 慶生
Celebrating A Birthday

 情境對話——和商務客／家庭客
3.1 的應答 1 Dialogue with Business
Customers / Family Guests 1 *Track 45*

 Waiter 服務生，簡稱 W。

 Guest, Mr. Brown 商務客，Brown 先生，簡稱 G。

The telephone is ringing...

R: Good afternoon, this is Happy Friday Restaurant. How may I help you?

G: Yes, I would like to know if there is any service provided for a birthday party?

R: Yes, sir. We provide the good places of our restaurant for our customers to meet their **purposes**.

G: Good. Could you briefly introduce the places and the related services for me?

R: No problem, sir. We provide indoor and outdoor spaces: the charge of the indoor service is cheaper than that of the outdoors. But we sometimes suggest our customers choose the places **depending** on their needs. Since you will be here to celebrate a birthday, the best **choice** that we will suggest is the outdoor place with the buffet meal services.

G: That sounds good. I would like to have the service quotation to make the decision.

R: Sure, we can provide the service quotation to you as you requested. How may I reach you?

G: Please send an email to me. My email address is danielbrown@jscor.com.

R: Ok, I will send the related information to you very soon.

G: Thank you.

R: You're welcome, sir. Please let me know if you decide to make a reservation. Have a nice day!

Unit 03

中文翻譯

電話鈴聲響起……

R：午安您好，這裡是快樂星期五餐廳。請問有我可以提您服務的地方嗎？

G：是的，我想要知道貴餐廳有沒有提供慶生服務？

R：有的，先生。我們餐廳有提供場地以供客戶的目的。

G：很好。可以麻煩你簡單介紹一下場地跟相關服務嗎？

R：沒問題，先生。我們提供室外及室內的場地，室內場地的價格會比室外場地來得便宜許多。但我們有時候會建議客人依照目的來選擇場地，由於您的目的是要慶生，因此最好的場地選擇，我們將會建議採室外場地搭配自助餐點的服務。

G：聽起來不錯。我想要服務的報價來考慮一下。

R：當然沒問題，我們可依您要求提供服務報價給您。請問怎麼提供給您服務報價呢？

G：請寄電子郵件給我，我的電子郵件信箱為 danielbrown@jscor.com.

R：好的，我將盡快將訊息郵寄給您。

G：謝謝你。

R：您別客氣，先生。若有需要訂位，再煩請讓我知道。祝您有美好的一天。

單字 Vocabulary

1. **purpose** *n.* 目的、宗旨
   例 I have no idea about his visiting purpose.
   我不曉得他來拜訪的目的是什麼。

2. **depend** *v.* 依賴、依靠
   例 You have to make your own choices instead of always depending on others.
   你必須要做出自己的選擇，而不是一直依賴別人的。

3. **choice** *n.* 選擇
   例 She has no choice but to leave.
   她別無選擇，只好離開。

3.2 情境對話──和商務客／家庭客的應答 2 Dialogue with Business Customers / Family Guests 2

 Track 46

 Receptionist 櫃台人員，簡稱 **R**。

 Guest, Mr. Brown 商務客／家庭客，*Brown* 先生，簡稱 **G**。

The telephone is ringing...

R: Good morning. This is Happy Friday Restaurant. How may I help you?

G: Yes, this is Mr. Brown. I would like to make a reservation for a birthday party.

R: Hello, Mr. Brown. It's great to hear from you again. When would you prefer for the birthday party?

G: In the evening on January 18 for about 30 people.

R: No problem. What kind of place would you like to book?

G: Outdoor spaces please.

R: And how about the meal? We serve the Italian buffet for that days' special.

G: No, thanks. I would like to choose the Plan A in the service package you sent to me yesterday.

R: No problem, sir. Then your reservation is confirmed.

G: Thank you. By the way, when is the deadline to pay the deposit?

R: One week before the day booked. How would you like to pay the deposit?

G: I'd like to have a transfer. Could you provide me the bank account of the restaurant?

R: There is a bank account shown on the quotation we sent to you yesterday.

G: Ok, I see. Thank you.

R: You're welcome, sir.

Unit 03

中文翻譯

電話鈴聲響起……

R：早安您好，這裡是快樂星期五餐廳。請問有我可以提供您服務的地方嗎？

G：是的，我是 Brown 先生。我想要預訂生日派對。

R：哈囉，Brown 先生。很開心再次聽到您的來電。您想要預定哪個時間的生日派對呢？

G：一月十八號晚上，大約三十人。

R：沒問題。您想預定怎麼樣的場地呢？

G：室外場地。

R：那餐點呢？我們當天有提供義式自助餐。

G：不用了，謝謝。我選擇昨天你寄給我的套裝服務裡的 A 計畫。

R：沒問題，先生。已確認您的訂位了。

G：謝謝你。對了，最後支付訂金的日期是哪一天呢？

R：是您預定日的前一週。您想用什麼方式支付訂金呢？

G：用轉帳的方式。煩請提供貴餐廳的銀行帳戶資訊。

R：您可以參考昨天的報價單上，有顯示我們的銀行帳戶資訊。

G：好，我瞭解了，謝謝。

R：您別客氣，先生。

單字 Vocabulary

1. **bank** *n.* 銀行

   例 The bank is robbed.
   這間銀行被搶了。

2. **account** *n.* 帳戶

   例 Please keep your bank account number safely.
   請小心保管您的銀行帳戶號碼。

3. **show** *v.* 展現

   例 He sent his girlfriend flowers to show his love for her.
   他送花給女友，展現他對她的愛。

 3.3 情境對話——和商務客／家庭客的應答 3 Dialogue with Business Customers / Family Guests 3

 Track 47

 Receptionist 櫃台人員，簡稱 R。

 Waiter 服務生，簡稱 W。

 Guest, Mr. Brown 商務客／家庭客，Brown 先生，簡稱 G。

Before the party starts...

R: Good evening, Mr. Brown.

G: Good evening. Is everything all well prepared?

R: Don't worry, sir. Everything is all well prepared.

G: Good.

R: There are going to be four waiters to assist you at the party if there is any need to be immediately provided.

G: Thank you.

R: You're welcome, sir. If there is any question or service that needs to be solved and provided, please let me know.

During the party...

G: Hey, excuse me. We need more cocktails and some ice cream; could you please bring me some?

W: Certainly sir. I'll be right back, please wait a second.

Checking the bill...

R: Hi, Mr. Brown. How was the party? Did everything go well?

G: The party was great and everybody had fun.

R: I'm glad to hear that. Are you going to pay the bill now?

G: Yes, please.

R: Ok. Here is the invoice for you. The **remaining** service fee after deducting the deposit you have prepaid earlier is $980, including the 10% sales tax. How would you like to make your payment?

G: By cash, please.

R: Ok. Thank you for choosing our restaurant. We hope to see you soon.

Unit 03

中文翻譯

派對開始前⋯⋯

R：晚安，Brown 先生。

G：晚安，一切都準備好了嗎？

R：別擔心，先生。一切都已就緒。

G：很好。

R：我們將會派四名服務生來協助派對的進行，若有任何需要，可以立即提供服務。

G：謝謝你。

R：您別客氣，先生。若有任何問題或服務需求，請讓我知道。

派對進行中⋯⋯

G：嘿，不好意思。我們需要來些雞尾酒及冰淇淋，可以幫我們拿一些過來嗎？

W：當然好的，先生。我稍會回來，請稍等。

結帳中⋯⋯

R：嗨，Brown 先生。派對還好嗎？一切都還順利嗎？

G：派對很棒，大家都玩得很愉快。

R：我很開心聽到您與貴賓們都玩得愉快。您要結帳了嗎？

G：是的，麻煩了。

R：好的，這是您的發票。扣掉您的訂金後，剩下應付服務費用為 980 元含 10% 銷售稅。您要怎麼支付呢？

G：現金。

R：好的。感謝您選擇本飯店，希望下次很快可以在為您服務。

Unit 03

單字 Vocabulary

1. remaining *adj.* 剩餘的

   例 The company is going to sell the remaining materials to another competitor.

   公司正打算將剩餘的原料賣給其他競爭者。

3.4 換句話說 In Other Words

There is a bank account info shown on the quotation we sent to you yesterday.

您可以參考昨天的報價單上，有顯示我們的銀行帳戶資訊。

☕ **Please refer to the quotation we sent to you yesterday for the bank information.**

請您參考昨天寄給您的報價單，上有銀行的資訊。

☕ **Please kindly refer to the quotation for the bank information.**

煩請您參考昨天寄給您的報價單，上有銀行的資訊。

☕ **For the bank information, please kindly refer to the quotation we sent to you yesterday.**

若您需要銀行資訊，煩請您請您參考昨天寄給您的報價單。

I will send the related information to you very soon.

我將盡快將訊息郵寄給您。

☕ **I will give you the message as soon as possible.**

我將盡快給您訊息。

☕ **The message will be sent to you very soon.**

這些訊息將會很快地寄給您。

☕ **I will do my best to provide the information for you**

我將盡我所能提供相關資訊給你。

I would like to know if there is any service provided for a birthday party?

我想要知道貴餐廳有沒有提供慶生服務？

Is there any space available for a party?
請問有空間提供給派對服務嗎？

Does the restaurant provide the meal and beverage for a party?
餐廳有提供派對服務食物及酒水嗎？

Is the party service available?
派對服務現在有提供嗎？

I would like to have the service quotation to make the decision.
我想要服務的報價來考慮一下。

I will take it if the price is good enough.
若價格好一點，我會購買。

I need to take a look of the service quotation and think about the service I need.
我要看一下服務的報價，想想看我需要的服務。

Could you please provide me the service quotation so that I can discuss with my wife?
你可以提供一個報價單給我嗎？這樣我才可以跟我老婆討論一下。

Unit 03

Unit 04 外燴 Catering Services

4.1 情境對話——和商務客／家庭客的應答 Dialogue with Business Customers / Family Guests

 Track 48

 Receptionist 櫃台人員，簡稱 **R**。

 Guest, Mr. Brown 商務客，Brown 先生，簡稱 **G**。

The telephone is ringing...

R: Good afternoon. This is Happy Friday Restaurant. How may I help you?

G: Yes, I would like to know if there are any catering services provided?

R: Yes, there are.

G: Good. Could you briefly introduce your **catering** plans to me?

R: No problem, sir. Our restaurant can provide you with the best catering services. We provide our customers many types of cuisines for their own choice. You can visit our website for the menu.

G: Sounds good. Please give me the website address.

R: Sure. The website **address** is www.happyfriday.com.

G: Thank you.

R: You're welcome, sir. Please let me know if you **decide** to make a reservation for catering. Have a nice day!

The phone is ringing again...

R: Good afternoon, this is Happy Friday Restaurant. How may I help you?

G: Yes. I would like to make a reservation for the catering service.

R: When would you like to have the catering service, sir?

G: I would like to have it on next Sunday afternoon from 12:00 pm.

R: Ok, let me check it.

Unit 04

One minute later...

R: Sir, we are sorry to tell you that our schedule for that Sunday is fully booked.

G: Ok, I see. Then I guess I need to try another one. Thank you.

中文翻譯

電話鈴聲響起……

R：午安您好，這裡是快樂星期五餐廳。請問有我可以提供您服務的地方嗎？

G：是的，我想要知道貴餐廳有沒有提供外燴服務？

R：有的，我們有提供。

G：很好。那麻煩請你為我簡單介紹您的外燴好嗎？

R：沒問題的，先生。我們餐廳能提供您最好的外燴服務。我們有提供許多種類的美食供我們的顧客來選擇。您可以到我們的網站上查詢菜單。

G：聽起來不錯。請提供我網站地址。

R：當然沒問題，網址是 www.happyfriday.com。

G：謝謝你。

R：您別客氣，先生。若您有需要預定外燴，再煩請讓我知道。祝您有美好的一天。

電話又響起……

R：您好，這裡是快樂星期五餐廳，請問有我可以供您服務的地方嗎？

G：我想要預訂外燴服務。

R：請問您想預定什麼時後呢？

G：我想預定下星期天下午 12:00 的外燴服務。

R：好的，讓我查一下。

一分鐘後……

R：先生，我們星期天的時間都被訂滿了。

G：好的，我瞭解了，我想我需要問問其它家了，謝謝您。

單字 Vocabulary

1. **catering** *n.* 外燴、承辦酒席

   例 We plan to order the catering service for the meeting next Monday.
   我們計畫為下週一的會議舉辦酒席。

2. **address** *n.* 地址

   例 Please fill out the address in the blank column.
   請在空白欄位填上地址。

3. **decide** *v.* 決定

   例 I haven't decided where to go.
   我還沒有決定要去哪。

Unit 04

4.2 情境對話——和家庭客的應答
Dialogue with Family Guests

 Track 49

Receptionist 櫃台人員，簡稱 R。

Guest, Mr. Brown 家庭客，Brown 先生，簡稱 G。

The telephone is ringing...

R: Good morning. This is Happy Friday Restaurant. How may I help you?

G: Yes, this is Mr. Brown. I would like to make a reservation for catering service.

R: Hello, Mr. Brown. It's great to hear from you again. When would you like to book for catering service?

G: June 18.

R: No problem, sir. What would you like for the catering service?

G: It is an outdoor party for approximately 100 people in my garden. I need the caterer to get the meal and beverages ready before the party begins.

R: No problem, sir. What kind of meal do you prefer?

G: What do you recommend?

R: We have three plans for the catering service. May I send the plan to you?

G: Sure.

R: Ok. Please give me your email address.

G: jasonbrown@hakll.com

R: No problem, sir.

G: Thank you. By the way, when is the deadline to pay the deposit?

R: One month before the day reserved. How would you like to pay the deposit?

G: I would like to make a transfer. Could you provide me the bank account of the restaurant?

R: Yes, sir. I will send the bank information with the plan to you later.

Unit 04

中文翻譯

電話鈴聲響起……

R：早安您好，這裡是快樂星期五餐廳。請問有我可以提您服務的地方嗎？

G：是的，我是 Brown 先生。我想要預訂外燴服務。

R：哈囉，Brown 先生。很開心再次聽到您的來電。您想要預定哪個時間的外燴服務呢？

G：六月十八號。

R：沒問題的，先生。您想要怎麼樣的外燴服務呢？

G：這是一場在我的花園裡舉行的派對，約莫有 100 人。我需要外燴師傅在派對開始前先準備好餐點及飲料。

R：沒問題，先生。那您比較傾向哪類型的餐點呢？

G：你建議怎樣？

R：我們針對外燴服務有三個方案。我可以寄給您參考嗎？

G：當然可以。

R：好的，請提供我您的電子郵件信箱。

G：jasonbrown@hakll.com。

R：沒問題的，先生。

G：謝謝你。對了，最後支付訂金的日期是哪一天呢？

R：是您預定日的前一個月。您想用什麼方式支付訂金呢？

G：用轉帳的方式。煩請提供貴餐廳的銀行帳戶資訊。

R：好的，先生。待會我將銀行資訊連同方案一起寄給您。

Unit 04

單字 Vocabulary

1. **garden** *n.* 花園

   例 There is a beautiful garden in the downtown.
   鬧區中有一個漂亮的花園。

4.3 情境對話──和團體客導遊的應答
Dialogue with Tour Guides

 Track 50

 Caterer 外燴師傅，簡稱 C。

 Receptionist 餐廳櫃台人員，簡稱 R。

 Tour Guide, Mr. Brown 導遊，Brown 先生，簡稱 T。

Before the party starts, the caterer and her crew start to prepare the meal and beverages.

C: Good morning, Mr. Brown.

T: Good morning. Is everything all well prepared?

C: Don't worry, sir. Everything is in the process of preparation now.

T: Good.

C: The food and beverages are **almost** well prepared, and I will send three waiters to assist the party.

T: Thank you.

C: You're welcome, sir. If there is any request, please kindly let me know.

Checking the bill... Mr. Brown just transferred the payment of catering; he is calling to the receptionist to double check the payment.

R: Hi, Mr. Brown. How was the catering? Was everything go well?

T: Yes, the food and beverages were great. Thanks for the assistance that you all provided that day.

R: You're welcome, sir. We're glad you had a great time.

T: By the way, I just transferred the payment of catering. Please confirm it.

R: Yes, sir. Please wait a second for confirmation.

T: Ok.

R: Yes, sir. The payment is confirmed. Thank you for choosing our restaurant. We hope to see you soon next time.

Unit 04

中文翻譯

派對開始前，外燴師傅及他的手下們開始準備餐點及飲料……

C：早安，Brown 先生。

T：早安，一切都準備好了嗎？

C：別擔心，先生。一切都在準備中。

T：很好。

C：餐點及飲料差不多準備好了，我將會派三位服務生來協助派對之進行。

T：謝謝你。

C：您別客氣，先生。若有其他需要服務的地方，請您讓我知道。

結帳中。Brown 先生剛將轉入外燴的餘款，他正在打電話給櫃檯確認帳款……

R：嗨，Brown 先生。外燴服務還好嗎？一切都還順利嗎？

T：是的，餐點及飲料都很棒。感謝你們那天提供的協助。

R：您別客氣，先生。我們替您感到開心。

T：對了，我剛才將剩餘的外燴服務費用轉帳過去了，麻煩確認一下。

R：好的，先生。請您稍等，我確認一下。

T：好。

R：先生，款項確認收到，謝謝。也感謝您選擇本餐廳，希望下次很快可以在為您服務。

單字 Vocabulary

1. **crew** *n.* 一組工作人員

   例 The maintenance crew will come to fix your car.
   維修人員將會過去維修您的車子。

2. **almost** *adv.* 幾乎、差不多

   例 We are almost here; please wait a second for us.
   我們就快到了，請等我們一下。

3. **confirm** *v.* 確認

   例 I will confirm the schedule with him again.
   我將會跟他再度確認一次行程。

Unit 04

4.4 換句話說 In Other Words

May I send the plan to you?

我可以將方案寄給您參考嗎？

Would you like to take a look of this plan for reference?
請問您想要看看此方案做參考嗎？

May I send the plan to you so that you can take a look of it?
可以容我將方案寄給您作參考嗎？

Would you like to refer to the plan?
請問您要參考此方案嗎？

We provide our customers many types of cuisine for their own choice. You can visit our website for the menu.

我們有提供許多種類的美食供顧客選擇。您可以到我們的網站上查詢菜單。

There are lots of delicious foods we provide. You can get more information about it on our website.
我們有提供許多美味食物。詳情請至我們網站。

You can go to our Facebook page to see more delicious food we provide.
你可以上我們的臉書粉絲團去看我們所提供的美食。

Please refer to our website for more information about our menu and related services.
請詳見我們的網站洽詢更多有關菜單及相關服務。

When would you like to have the catering service?

您想要預定哪個時間的外燴服務呢？

When would you like to have the catering service?

您想要哪個時間來外燴服務呢？

When would you like the catering service to start?

你想要預訂什麼時候的外燴服務呢？

What's the time that you would like to have the catering service?

你想要什麼時候的外燴服務呢？

What would you like the catering service?

您想要怎麼樣的外燴服務呢？

Do you have any ideas about the catering service?

你對外燴服務有什麼想法嗎？

What do you plan for your catering service?

對於外燴服務，你有想法嗎？

What kind of catering services would you like?

您想要怎麼樣的外燴服務呢？

Unit 05 生機飲食展 Organic Food Show

5.1 情境對話──生機飲食集團 CEO 和營運長的討論 A discussion about the Preparation of the Organic Show

 Track 51

*President, Mary Harris 自然生機飲食總裁，Mary Harris 女士，簡稱 **P**。*

*CEO, John Smith 自然生機飲食營運長，John Smith 先生，簡稱 **C**。*

The government is promoting natural organic food due to the increasing awareness of environmental protection; many food manufacturers and agricultural experts are invited to attend the 2016 National Natural Organic Show in Taipei. The Home Made Factory, the most famous natural organic food manufacturer is also invited and Mary Harris, the president of the Home Made Factory, is directing her CEO, John Smith, to present her the detailed information of the show.

P: John, I need to know the process of how you are going to conduct the food show.

C: Absolutely, Mary. We plan to set up our exhibition booths three days before the show and here is the daily schedule during the show. On the first day, we are going to release our brand new organic products and will provide some free samples to the first 20 guests who join our opening ceremony.

P: That's a good plan. How about the second day and the last day?

C: Based on prior experience, we will make a change on the second day this year. We will invite our clients, Big Mama Italian Home Made Restaurant, to present our products by showing their classic Italian cuisine recipes and hold a free organic food party for the participants.

P: Sounds good. And on the third day?

C: As usual, we will have an on-sale party and the coupons will be delivered to the organizers this afternoon and we will release the related information on our website and the newspapers.

P: You've done a good job, John.

C: Thanks, Mary.

P: Ok, I will see you then.

C: Ok.

中文翻譯

政府現在正在推行生機飲食，主要因為是對於環境保護意識之興起。許多食品製造商及農業專家被邀請參加於台北舉行的 2016 年國家自然生機飲食展。**Home Made Factory** 是一家極具知名的自然生機飲食製造商，為受邀廠商之一。**Mary Harris** 是 **Home Made Factory** 的總裁，正在指示公司營運長 **John Smith** 一些有關參展之流程細節。

P：John，我需要知道你將會怎麼進行食品展的流程。

C：當然沒問題了，總裁。我們計畫在食品展舉行的前三天佈置展場攤位，這個是食品展期間的每日行事曆。第一天，我們將會發佈有機新品上市的消息，並且提供一些免費試吃品給前 20 位參與我們攤位開幕典禮的民眾。

P：這計畫很好。那第二天與最後一天呢？

C：依照以往的經驗，我們今年將會於第二天做個改變。我們將會邀請我們的客戶，Big Mama 義式手作料理餐廳，透過他們經典義式食譜來呈現我們公司的產品，提供參與者一個免費的有機美食餐會。

P：聽起來很好。那第三天呢？

C：與往常一樣，我們將會舉辦特賣會，折價券將會於今天下午送至主辦單位那邊，以及我們會透過我們公司網站及報紙來釋出相關訊息。

P：John，你做得很好。

C：謝謝總裁，我只是做好分內工作。

P：那麼待會見了。

C：好的。

單字 Vocabulary

1. **organic** *adj.* 有機的
   例 Many people are trying to experience the organic food lifestyle to make a healthier life.
   許多人嘗試著體驗有機飲食的生活方式來使生活更健康。

2. **awareness** *n.* 意識
   例 Due to the unusual flood last week, the residents' awareness about the global environment is enhanced.
   由於上禮拜不尋常的水災，讓居民們更加強了全球環境意識。

3. **agricultural** *adj.* 農業的
   例 Mary is an agricultural expert in the organic field.
   Mary 是一位在生機領域的農業專家。

5.2 情境對話——和家庭客的應答
Dialogue with Family Guests

 Track 52

Salesman of Home Made Factory
自然生機飲食的銷售員，簡稱 **S**。

Guest, Ms. Jackson 家庭客，*Jackson* 小姐，簡稱 **G**。

It's the opening day of the 2016 National Natural Organic Show. The new arrival products of Home Made Factory are being promoted very well and attract many potential customers to take a try on their products.

S: Hello, madam. This is our brand-new product; it's 100% organic olive oil and all the raw materials are from France. Would you like to try some?

G: Sure. How can I use it?

S: You can use it anytime, but you can't use it to cook deep fried food. We are now providing a very **exclusive** discount to our new client; once you buy one bottle, you can get a free one or the similar product with the same price. And once you become a member of our Organic Life Society, you will receive the discount **coupon** in the first month of each quarter and with no **expiration** date.

G: Ok, I'll take it.

S: Thank you, madam. Please come with me for further information.

G: Yes. Thank you. I have a catalogue of your products from your staff. I'm thinking maybe you will have recipes about how to use the olive oil?

S: Yes, we do. I'll get you some pamphlets. We also have tutorial videos online. It's highly recommended for our customers to watch the videos. Those videos will help you understand the recipes a lot.

G: Sounds great. Please do give me the address for the tutorial videos.

S: Sure, it is homemadefactory.com. You have to register first to get access to those videos.

G: Ok, I got it.

中文翻譯

今天就是 2016 年國家自然生機飲食展。**Home Made Factory** 新上市的產品被促銷的很好，吸引許多潛在的消費者前來試用他們的產品。

S：哈囉，女士。這是我們新上市的產品，是百分之百有機橄欖油，所有的原料都來自法國喔。您要試看看嗎？

G：當然好囉，我要怎麼使用呢？

S：您可以在任何時候使用，除了用油炸的方式烹調外。我們現在提供給我們新顧客一個很優惠的價格，您買一罐橄欖油，即可以免費獲得一罐同樣的橄欖油，或是同價位的類似商品一件。若您成為我們有機生活社團的會員，您將於每季的第一個月收到折價券，而且是無使用期限的唷。

G：好，那我要買。

S：謝謝您，女士。更多詳細資訊，請跟我這邊請。

G：好的，謝謝您。我剛從您的同仁拿到一本產品目錄，我在想您們有沒有如何使用橄欖油料理的食譜。

S：我們有的。我幫您拿幾本手冊，我們也有線上教學影片，也會強烈建議我們的顧客能觀看影片。這些影片能幫您多多了解食譜的。

G：聽起來很步錯，那麻煩您給我影片的網址。

S：網址是 homemadefactory.com，您要先註冊才能觀看影片喔。

G：好的，我了解了。

單字 Vocabulary

1. **exclusive** *adj.* 優的、獨家的

   例 All the exclusive information can be found on this website.
   所有獨家資訊都可以在這個網站上找到。

2. **coupon** *n.* 優惠券

   例 The best way to save your money is to use coupons.
   使用優惠券是最省錢的方式。

3. **expiration** *n.* 使用期限

   例 The product is much cheaper than usual because of its expiration date.
   因為使用期限的關係，這個產品賣得比平常還便宜。

5.3 情境對話——和團體客導遊的應答
Dialogue with Tour Guides

 Track 53

 The one who is in charge of the stand in the exhibition 展場攤位負責人，簡稱 T。

 Tour Guide, Helen Jackson 導遊，Helen Jackson 小姐，簡稱 T。

 Tourist 遊客，簡稱 T。

T: Hello, may I help you?

T: Yes, I'm Helen Jackson. I'm the travel guide of Happy Holiday Travel Agency. I booked a morning tour for my guests two days ago.

T: Yes. You have 15 guests, right?

T: Yes.

T: Please come with me, madam.

(The one who is in charge of the stand in the exhibition leads the group into the standand start to speak.)

T: Hello everyone, I'm the one who is in charge of the stand today. First of all, welcome come here and have a great time.

There are many newly **released** products on the **shelves**. You can try and taste them all. And there, the table next to the door, product brochures are available for your **reference**. If you have any questions about our products, please just ask the nearest salesman. We wish you a pleasant time here!

T: Excuse me. I would like to know more about the fresh organic olive oil.

T: Sure. Could you please wait a minute, I'll get some samples for you.

One minute later...

T: Ok, this olive oil is our newly released product. It's 100% made in Italy; genuinely organic. We are now promoting this oil for the group tourists. Once you buy two bottles, we will send you the samples of our new arrivals.

T: Great.

中文翻譯

T：您好，請問有需要幫忙嗎？

T：有的，我是 Helen Jackson，快樂假期旅行公司的導遊。我前兩天有為我的團員預定今天早上的場次。

T：是的，共 15 位嗎？

T：是的。

T：請跟我這邊來，女士。

（展場負責人帶領整團旅客進入展場，並且開始發言……）

T：哈囉，大家好。我是今天展場負責人。首先，歡迎各位來到這邊與我們同歡。我們這邊有許多新上架的產品，全部都可試用、試吃。以及，門口旁邊有張桌子，上面有產品手冊供大家拿取、參考。若您有任何想問的問題，請洽離您最近的銷售人員。我們祝您有個美好的時光。

T：不好意思，我想要多了解一點這款新鮮有機橄欖油。

T：當然好的，請您稍等，我去拿些試用品給您。

一分鐘後……

T：好的，這款橄欖油是我們最新發售的產品，他是百分之百義大利製，
全採用有機原料製成。我們現在有替團體旅客做這款油的促銷活
動，買兩罐油，未來我們將會寄送新產品給您試用。

T：真好，那我要兩罐。

單字 Vocabulary

1. **release** *v.* 釋出
   例 The company released the news that they were facing the
   financial crises.
   公司對外釋出消息表示公司正面臨財務危機。

2. **shelf** *n.* 架子
   例 Mom put the dangerous tools on the shelves to prevent my
   baby brother from touching them accidentally.
   媽媽將危險的工具放到架子上，以避免我弟弟接觸到。

3. **reference** *n.* 參考
   例 Find more information, please see the reference here.
   找更多資訊，請參閱這裡。

5.4 換句話說 In Other Words

I need to know the process of how you are going to conduct the food show.
我需要知道你將會怎麼進行食品展的流程。

I would like to know the plan for the food show.
我想要到食品展的計畫是什麼。

Could you elaborate the process of the food show?
你可以說明一下食品展的流程嗎？

What is plan for food show that you will run next week?
針對下禮拜的食品展，你的流程計畫為何？

We plan to set up our exhibition booths three days before the show day and here is the daily schedule during the show.
我們計畫在食品展舉行的前三天佈置展場攤位，這個是食品展期間的每日行事曆。

We will decorate the booths and plan to begin three days before the show; I can show you the detailed schedule.
我們將會佈置展場，計畫是在秀展開始的前三天開始弄，我可以給你看詳細的計畫表。

Here is the schedule for the show; we will begin the decoration three days before the show.
這是食品展的計畫表，我們將會在食品展開始前三天開始著手佈置。

Here is the plan for the start up preparation; we will do it three days before the opening of the show.

這是佈置展場的計畫表，我們將於秀展開幕會的前三天著手佈置。

Based on prior experience, we will make a change on the second day this year.

依照以往的經驗，我們今年將會於第二天做個改變。

On the basis of our prior experience, we will change the schedule for the second day of the show.

根據以往的經驗，我們改變秀展第二天的行程。

We will change the activity on the second day according to our experience in the past years.

我們將會根據以前年度的經驗，來改變第二天的活動。

The plan for the second day of the show will be changed based on the experiences we have.

秀展第二天的計畫將會根據我們有的經驗來做改變。

Unit 06 推廣蔬食 Promoting Vegetarian Food

6.1 情境對話——生機飲食集團 CEO 和餐廳員工的討論 A discussion about the Preparation of Promoting Vegetarian Food

 Track 54

CEO, Henry Woods 自然生機飲食總裁，
Henry Woods 先生，簡稱 C。

CEO's subordinates, Jack 自然生機飲食營運長的下屬，
Jack 先生、May 小姐，簡稱 S。

More and more people around the world now are now promoting the advantages of health diet, especially vegetarian food. It's easier to find a vegetarian restaurant than it was many years ago. But there is a growing concern about the vegetarian diet that may not provide sufficient nutrition to meet daily basic needs. Fresh Diet Restaurant, a newly opened vegetarian restaurant, is trying to promote the upside of being a vegan who is free of worries about the lack of nutrition sources and would like to bring the potential vegetarian customers newer and much more creative cuisine made of organic vegetables and fruits. The CEO, Henry Woods, are having a meeting with his subordinates, discussing the activity which will be held in World Trade Center next week. In the exhibition, their new dish will be released and the first 50 guests will have the chance to get a free vegetarian meal.

C: Ok, guys. I think you all know about how important the activity is next week in the World Trade Center. I would like to know, before the preparations for the project are all confirmed, do you have any other suggestions?

S: Mr. Woods, I have an idea.

C: Go ahead, Jack.

S: We can invite the guests who are interested in our products to be one of our Eating Good, Eating Health members; they will receive the weekly e-newsletter about the health information and also we can provide some coupons to them, so they can use the coupons to buy our products and dishes at our online store.

C: That's good, Jack. You are in charge of this part now. Anything else?

S: Sir, as mentioned by Jack, it's better to release this information on our website or in the newspaper in advance.

Unit 06

C: Yes, the earlier the information is released, the more potential customers we can have. Ok, guys, be sure you need to promote the upside and spirit of being a vegetarian and how good it is to eat healthier, not just promote our products only.

中文翻譯

在全球，愈來愈多人在推廣健康飲食的好處，特別是蔬食飲食。相較於幾年前，現在你可以輕易地找到蔬食餐廳了。但，關於蔬食飲食是否可以提供足夠的營養已符合每日基礎所需，還是有不少人存疑。**Fresh Diet Restaurant** 是一間新開幕的蔬食餐廳，試著推廣成為蔬食者的好處，而且吃素的人可不需擔心缺乏營養來源；餐廳也想透過更多有機蔬果所烹煮的創意料理來帶來更多潛在的客人。**Fresh Diet Restaurant** 的營運長 **Henry Woods**，正與他的下屬們開會，討論下週將在世貿中心舉辦的活動；有道新料理將於該展覽發佈、上市，前五十名賓客將機會獲得免費蔬食一份。

C：好的，夥伴們。我想你們應該都了解下週在世貿中心舉辦的活動有多麼的重要。我想知道，在提案確認前，你們還有什麼建議嗎？

S：我有一個想法。

C：繼續說，Jack。

S：我們可以邀請那些對我們公司產品有興趣的賓客成為我們社團的一員，他們將會於每週收到電子報，裡面有健康資訊內容提供給他們，並且有提供一些折價券，讓他們可以在我們網路商店購物時使用。

C：這點子很好。Jack，這一塊，你現在是主要負責人了。其他人還有嗎？

S：有的，如同 Jack 剛才所說，我們最好現在發布訊息到網站及報紙上。

C：沒錯，愈早讓這消息發佈出去，會增加更多我們潛在的顧客。好吧，各位，請確認你們必須推廣成為蔬食者的好處，以及吃得更健康的好處為何，別只是推銷我們的產品而已。

單字 Vocabulary

1. **advantage** *n.* 好處、優點
   例 The advantage of being a member of our club is that you can get a free 15ml sample of the new arrival product.
   成為我們俱樂部會員的好處是，您可以免費獲得 15 毫升的新產品。

2. **vegetarian** *adj.* 蔬食的
   例 You can be a smart vegetarian to choose what you eat.
   你可以當個聰明的蔬食者來選擇要吃的食物。

3. **concern** *n.* 顧慮
   例 He has made up his mind to do it by himself without any concern.
   他已下定決心，無任何顧慮，靠著自己的力量。

情境對話──和家庭客的應答
Dialogue with Family Guests

 Project Manager 自然生機飲食的專案經理，簡稱 **P**。

 Coordinator 自然生機飲食的專員，簡稱 **C**。

 Guest, Ms. Lee 家庭客，*Lee* 小姐，簡稱 **G**。

Before the conference starts...

P: Good morning ladies and gentlemen. Welcome to Fresh Diet Restaurant. Later, we are going to present you with our vision in the vegetarian food field and the latest products which are going to be released. If you have any questions or are interested in our products, our sales **coordinator** will provide you with further information.

After the conference...

C: Hello, madam. How may I help you?

G: Yes, I would like to buy this set of products. I want to know more about the nutrition sources if I choose to eat lightly.

C: Sure. Here are the **instructions** for the dieter or for people who want to eat lightly. For daily basic **nutrition**, you can eat our purely organic blueberry cereal with low fat milk or soy milk. At the beginning of the diet, I suggest you eat whole wheat bread or oat bread with the cereals at the same time.

G: I see. Just follow the diet instructions.

C: Basically yes, madam. You can find the solution through reading the instructions. The customer service number is on the back of instructions. If you have further information, you can contact us. How would you like to pay?

G: Credit card.

C: No problem, madam. Here is your receipt. Thank you so much!

G: By the way, do you have an official website? I'm thinking if I could get any further information there. It's faster as well too, you know.

C: Yes, we do. It is freshdiet.com. We also have a fan page on Facebook. Please do give us some likes. It will be our greatest support.

Unit 06

中文翻譯

說明會開始前……

P：早安，女士及先生們。歡迎來到 Fresh Diet Restaurant，待會，我們將要向你呈現我們公司在蔬食領域的願景，以及即將推出的新產品。若您有其他的問題想詢問，或是對我們的產品有進一步的興趣，我們的銷售專員將會為您提供更多的資訊。

說明會過後……

C：女士您好，有什麼我可以幫忙您的嗎？

G：有的，我想要買這組產品。若我選擇清淡飲食的話，我想知道更多有關營養來源的訊息。

C：當然囉。這是給您的使用指南，專門給節食者或想要吃得更輕盈的人。為了提供每日基礎的營養，您可以吃純有機藍莓穀片搭配低脂鮮奶或豆漿。在控制飲食初期，我建議您可以吃全麥麵包或燕麥麵包來搭配穀片。

G：我瞭解了，就是照著使用指南走就是了。

C：基本上是的，女士。您可以在使用指南上找到問題的解答。使用指南的背面有顧客服務電話，若您有進一步的問題，可以與我們聯絡。您要怎麼付款呢？

G：用信用卡。

C：沒問題，女士。這是您的收據，非常謝謝您。

G：對了，請問您們有官網嗎？我在想我是不是有可能從那取得進一步的資訊，這樣也比較快，對吧？

C：有的，我們的網址是 freshdiet.com.，我們也有臉書粉絲團，也請您多多幫我們按讚，這會是我們最大的支持。

單字 Vocabulary

1. **coordinator** *n.* 專員
   例 The sales coordinator has a good skill to persuade the lady to buy his product.
   這個銷售專員有很好的技巧來說服那位女士購買他的產品。

2. **instruction** *n.* 使用說明
   例 Please follow the instructions on the bottle before taking the medicine.
   當您服藥時請按照瓶罐上的使用說明。

3. **nutrition** *n.* 營養
   例 Salmon is rich in a lot of nutrition, so you have to try one.
   鮭魚富含營養，所以你必須要試試。

6.3 情境對話——和團體客導遊的應答
Dialogue with Tour Guides

 Track 56

 The salesman of the stand 展場攤位銷售員，簡稱 **S**。

 The manager who is in charge of the stand in the exhibition 展場攤位負責人，簡稱 **M**。

 Tour Guide, Jane 導遊，Jane 小姐，簡稱 **T**。

The travel tour guide, Jane, is going to bargain over the product prices with the manager taking in charge of the stand of the exhibition.

S: Hello madam, how may I help you?

T: Yes, I would like to talk to the one who is in charge of this stand.

S: Ok, what's the matter?

T: My travel group is willing to buy the newly released products, but they are wondering if they could have a discount or not.

S: I'm sorry, madam. We only provide discounts for the products that are not newly released.

T: I understand, but they promise to buy the entire stock now in the exhibition.

S: I'll have to ask the manager.

T: Sure, thank you so much, and I will be right here to wait for your response.

Ten minutes later...

S: Madam, our manager will see you later and make a deal with you about the price. Please wait.

Five minutes later...

M: Hi, I'm Philip, the manager. How can I help you? I heard you would like to bargain over the price.

T: Yes, my travel group members would like to buy the entire stock you **currently** have, and they would like to use the cheaper price to buy them. They want to have a 25% discount.

M: The lowest price we offer is 15% off of the total price.

T: How about 20% off? They are potential customers who are very likely to promote your products if they like them.

M: Ok. Deal!

中文翻譯

旅行社導遊 Jane 正要去與展場負責經理進行產品價格的商談。

S：哈囉，女士，請問我可以幫您什麼忙嗎？

T：有的，我想要要和展場負責人談一談。

S：好的，請問是什麼事呢？

T：我的團員們有意願要買新推出的產品，但是他們不知道能不能有折扣。。

S：我很抱歉，女士。我們只針對原有的產品進行價格折扣。

T：我了解，但他們保證將會購進現場所有的庫存。

S：我必須要問一下今天負責展場的經理。

T：當然囉，非常謝謝你，我會在那邊等你的回覆。

十分鐘後……

S：女士，我們經理等一下會跟您碰面，來討論產品價格問題，請稍等一下。

五分鐘後……

M：嗨，您好，我是這邊的經理，飛利浦。請問有什麼我可以效勞的嗎？我聽說，針對價格的部分，您想討論一下。

T：是的，我旅行社團員想要用較便宜的價格，來買你們現場庫存的產品，他們提出來的價格是打七五折。

M：我們最低能接受的價格是總價的八五折。

T：八折呢？他們真的是很潛力的顧客，只要他們喜歡您們的產品，他們就會幫忙推廣。

M：好的，成交。

單字 Vocabulary

1. **bargain** *v.* 議價
   例 Mom would like to bargain over the cheaper price with the salesperson.
   媽媽想要跟銷售人員議價一個便宜的價格。

2. **currently** *adv.* 目前地
   例 Due to the financial crisis of this company, the stock price currently decreases.
   股價最近下跌是因為這間公司的財務危機所致。

6.4 換句話說 In Other Words

I think you all know about how important the activity is next week in the World Trade Center.

我想你們應該都了解下週在世貿中心舉辦的活動有多麼的重要。

☕ You all know it's important for us to attend the activity next week.

你們全部都知道下禮拜的活動堆我們來說很重要。

☕ I guess you all know the upcoming activity is really a big event to our company.

我猜你們都知道即將到來的活動對我們公司來說是個大事件。

☕ I think you all understand that it's the most important event of the year.

我想你們都了解，這是本年度最重要的事件。

It's better to release this information on our website or in the newspaper in advance.

我們最好現在發布訊息到網站及報紙上。

☕ We can release the related information through the website and advertisements in the newspapers.

我們可以透過網路及報紙上的廣告來發佈相關訊息。

☕ All the information can be released to the public by our official website and advertisements in the newspapers.

所有的訊息可以在我們的官方網站上或是報紙廣告上發布。

The public will receive our information by mail.

大眾將會透過寄件信件的方式獲得我們的資訊。

Be sure you need to the upside and spirit of being a vegetarian and how good it is to eat healthier, not just promote our products only.

請確認你們必須推廣成為蔬食者的好處，以及吃得更健康的好處為何，別只是推銷我們的產品而已。

Make sure you all understand that not only selling our products is our mission but also promoting the upside of eating smarter and healthier.

請確認你們都了解，我們的任務不只是銷售商品，推廣聰明吃、健康吃也是任務之一。

I want you understand that you have to promote our products by presenting the advantage of being a smart dieter.

我想讓你們了解，你們必須藉由呈現聰明飲食者的好處來推廣我們的產品。

We would like to promote the advantage of being a vegetarian by introducing our products.

我們想要藉由我們的產品來歸廣成為蔬食者的好處。

Unit 07 參與外國美食展行銷台灣 Attending the Foreign Cuisine Exhibition and Introducing Taiwan

7.1 情境對話——食品集團 CEO 和餐廳員工的 討論 A discussion about the Preparation of the Foreign Cuisine Exhibition

 Track 57

 CEO of The Old Treefood, Jason Wang
老樹食品營運長，Jason Wang 先生，簡稱 **C**。

 Staff of The Old Treefood, Amy, Katy, Many
老樹食品的員工，Amy、Katy、Mandy 小姐，簡稱 **S**。

All the members of the food industry in Taiwan is planning to attend the annual foreign cuisine exhibition which will be held in Venice, Italy. The government will select the best food companies in the exhibition and give it a chance to take a part into the international cuisine event with its awarded food that can represent Taiwan and Taiwanese culture the most. After the selection, *The Old Treefood* company prevailed over other competitors and are so excited about this opportunity. Jason Wang, the CEO of *The OldTree*, is discussing the whole details with his subordinates.

C: Hey guys, I'm so glad to pronounce to you that our company has been selected to participate in the Foreign Cuisine Exhibition. As you know, we have made our efforts for several years; we have been trying to use the local ingredients to present the new and creative Taiwanese cuisine without losing the traditional and local flavors. We have found the old and really traditional **recipe** to keep the origin of the Taiwanese cuisine, and this is the best time to show the worldwide people our culture via those cuisines. So now, you can **propose** some ideas about this project or any idea you want to share.

S: Sir, about the cuisine, there are many different types of cuisine in any one of the counties here in Taiwan. I suggest we choose the best four cities and counties that are well known among the foreigners, and present the local cuisines and the related local traditions. That will attract the foreigners to come to our booths for further information.

C: That's a good idea. Anyone else?

S: We can hold an event in which we could **interact** with the people and also we can make some hand-made traditional sweets and cakes as a gift to the people who join our activity.

C: Katy's idea is good. And how about the set-up of the exhibition?

Unit 07

S: We can decorate the booth in the exhibition with the Taiwanese style, for instance, we can design a map of Taiwan and locate the major cities on the map, and the related brief introduction of the major cities can be presented on the side of the map.

中文翻譯

台灣的食品業正在計畫參加在義大利威尼斯舉辦的年度國外美食展。政府機關將從食品業者中挑選出一最佳的食品公司來代表參加這個國際年度饗宴，並讓食品公司用具代表性的台灣美食來呈現台灣在地文化。經過政府的挑選，老樹食品公司打敗其他競爭者，獲得了參展機會。他們非常興奮這次的參展機會，他們的營運長，**Jason Wang**，正與他的下屬們討論參展細節。

C：大夥們！我非常開心在這邊向大家宣佈，我們公司奪得參加國外美食展的機會。你們都知道，我們努力了好幾年，用傳統的食材來呈現新的極具創意的台灣美食，又不失傳統及在地的口味。我們有尋找出道地傳統的老食譜以及保留台灣美食的原汁原味，同時，這是向世界各地的人們介紹台灣文化的最佳時刻。所以現在，你們可以針對這個提案來提出建議或任何想分享的點子。

S：有關美食的部分，在台灣各地有不同的在地美食。我建議，可以選擇台灣最具盛名的四個城市，來呈現在地美食及相關的在地傳統文化，這將會吸引外國人到我們的攤位來瞭解更多的資訊。

C：這點子很好，還有人要發表意見嗎？

S：我們可以舉辦一個活動來與現場的人們互動，我們可以準備一些手作傳統甜點及蛋糕來給參與活動的朋友，當作是一個禮物。

C：Katy 的想法很棒。那展場的佈置呢？

S：我們可以用台灣風來佈置攤位，舉例來說，我們可以設計一個台灣地圖，並將主要城市在這個地圖上標示出來，並將主要城市的相關簡介在地圖旁邊呈現出來。

Unit 07

單字 Vocabulary

1. **annual** *adj.* 年度的

   例 The annual year end party is coming; all the subordinates in the company are looking forward to it.
   年度尾牙即將到來，公司所有員工都很期待參加。

2. **foreign** *adj.* 外國的

   例 We like to taste foreign cuisine, especially Italian food.
   我們喜歡品嚐外國料理，特別是義式料理。

註：其它單字請詳見 7.2。

7.2 情境對話——和家庭客的應答
Dialogue with Family Guests

 Track 58

Staff of The Old Treefood, Mandy 老樹食品的員工，Mandy 小姐，簡稱 S。

Guest 參展客，簡稱 G。

The host of Foreign Cuisine Exhibition is introducing Taiwan and its culture. Many people who come here to know more about Taiwan are interested in the traditional Taiwanese cuisines. Mandy, the one in charge of marketing, is trying to convince the participants to attend their activity.

S: Hello, welcome to our activity. Would you like to know more about Taiwanese culture? The activity that we provide is for you to get more information about traveling in Taiwan and also you will get a gift if you join. The gift contains the traditional Taiwanese sweets and cakes; it's really genuine; you have to try it!

G: Oh really! That's great. I have been interested in Taiwanese culture since I was a high school student. It's really a good chance to know more about Taiwan. I want to try some real Taiwanese food, you know, there are some Chinese restaurants in Italy, but it is difficult to find a real Taiwanese restaurant here.

S: Then you have to try it now! Welcome, sir. You can taste the food here, all you can eat. Stinky tofu, Spring rolls, Fried dumplings, Beef noodle soup...etc., you can find whatever you like in our booths.

G: Thanks!

S: We also hold some activities for guests to our booth. If you win one of them, you will have discount coupons available for the restaurant that is going to open up in Italy this July.

G: Sounds great.

S: Just take your time to look around and enjoy your Taiwanese cuisine time here!

Unit 07

中文翻譯

國外美食展的主持人正在介紹台灣及台灣文化。許多來這邊瞭解更多台灣資訊的人，都對傳統台灣美食很有興趣。行銷負責人 **Mandy**，正試著說服參與者來加入活動。

S：哈囉，歡迎參與我們的活動。想要瞭解更多的台灣文化嗎？我們提供了活動，讓您可以瞭解更多在台灣旅遊的訊息，以及您參與活動即可獲得一個禮物。禮物內容包含傳統台灣甜點及蛋糕，這真的很道地喔，您必須試看看！

G：噢，真的嗎！太棒了。我從還是個高中生時，就對台灣文化很感興趣。這真是認識台灣的絕佳機會。我想嚐看看道地的台灣美食，你知道，在義大利有很多中式料理餐廳，但要在這裡找到台式餐廳還真是不容易呢！

S：那麼您現在就必須嘗試看看了！歡迎您的參與，先生！您可以品嚐這裡所有的食物，臭豆腐、春捲、煎餃、牛肉湯麵等，您可以在我們攤位上找到您想吃的！

G：謝謝！

S：我們也有為來到我們攤位的顧客舉辦活動，如果您在活動中獲勝了，就能取得折價券，並可在今年七月於義大利開張的新餐廳使用。

G：聽起來真不錯。

S：那麼請您慢慢逛，也好好享受台灣的美食吧。

單字 Vocabulary

1. **recipe** *n.* 食譜

   例 Mom has her own recipe; she won't tell anybody how to cook the dish.

   媽媽有私房食譜，她不會透露給任何人如何做這道菜。

2. **interact** *v.* 互動

   例 It's really important to interact with others in the communicating generation.

   在這個溝通的世代，與他人互動是很重要的事。

3. **propose** *v.* 提出

   例 Anyone can propose their ideas about this project.

   任何人都可以針對這個提案提出想法。

Unit 07

7.3 情境對話——和團體客導遊的應答
Dialogue with Tour Guides

Track 59

 The salesman of the stand 展場攤位銷售員，簡稱 **S**。

 Tour Guide, Emily 導遊，Emily 小姐，簡稱 **T**。

 Tourist, Tom 遊客，Tom 先生，簡稱 **T**。

S: Hello, how may I help you?

T: Yes, I'm Emily, the tour guide of Big Apple Travel Agency.

S: Oh, hello, Emily. So, is your group ready to enter the exhibition now?

T: Yes.

S: Ok, please follow me this way.

T: Ok, everybody, we are going inside now. Please keep close.

The salesman leads the group into the exhibition.

S: Hello, welcome to our activity here. As you are the **privileged** customers, our company offers the best and ideal combo of our newly released products. Founded in Taiwan, we are a company that produces Taiwanese food and provides various types of Taiwanese high quality delicious cuisine. The following activities will provide every participant an opportunity to know more about the Taiwanese culture and foods, of course. I believe you all will have a good time here with us. Enjoy!

The group members are now taking in part of activities and testing the foods.

T: Excuse me. I would like to know whether the stinky tofu is available for sale here.

S: Yes, the frozen stinky tofu is available for sale. Do you like it?

T: Yeah, it tastes good although its smell is really stinky.

S: Just like its name, right?

T: I think it's pretty worthy to try. I would like to buy some for my family. My son had been to Taiwan once, and he told me the stinky tofu brought him the best memory about Taiwan. I think he would be happy to taste it again.

S: Sure it is, sir. How much you would like to buy?

中文翻譯

S：哈囉，請問有需要我幫忙嗎？

T：有的，我是大蘋果旅行社的導遊。

S：噢，哈囉，艾蜜莉。那麼，旅客都準備要進入展場了嗎？

T：是的。

S：好的，請跟我這邊來。

T：好的，各位，我們要走囉，跟緊一點喔。

銷售員帶領團體進入會場⋯⋯

S：哈囉，歡迎參與我們的活動。各位貴賓是我們的尊榮賓客，我們公司有提供最好及最理想的新產品組合給各位。我們公司是一間台灣的食品製造商，提供高品質的美味台灣美食。接下來各位會參與的活動，都有提供機會讓您了解更多台灣文化，當然也有美食品嚐囉。我相信各位在這裡會玩得很開心，祝您們玩得愉快。

團體旅客正在玩活動及品嚐美食……

T：不好意思，我想要知道，臭豆腐是不是在這裡可以買的到呢？

S：可以的，冷凍臭豆腐是買的到的。先生很喜歡對嗎？

T：對呀，很好吃，即使它聞起來真的很臭。

S：如其所名，對吧？

T：我認為這很值得品嘗。我想買一些給我家人常嚐。我兒子曾經到過台灣，他說這是對台灣最美好的回憶。我想他應該會很開心可以再次吃到臭豆腐。

S：一定是的。您想要買多少臭豆腐呢？

Unit 07

單字 Vocabulary

1. **privileged** *adj.* 尊榮的 特權的
   例 This service is only for the privileged customer.
   這項服務只提供給尊榮賓客。

2. **quality** *n.* 品質
   例 This company provides the products of high quality.
   這間公司提供高品質的產品。

7.4 換句話說 In Other Words

I'm so glad to pronounce to you that our company has been selected to participate in the Foreign Cuisine Exhibition.
我非常開心在這邊向大家宣佈，我們公司奪得參加國外美食展的機會。

☕ **I'm so happy to let you all know that we got the chance to attend the Foreign Cuisine Exhibition.**
我非常開心地告訴你們大家，我們公司奪得參加國外美食展的機會。

☕ **I'm here to pronounce to you that it's really an honor to attend the Foreign Cuisine Exhibition.**
我在這邊向大家宣佈，能夠參與這次國外美食展真是一項殊榮。

☕ **Our company is going to be one of the participants of Foreign Cuisine Exhibition.**
我們公司將成為國際美食展的參與廠商之一員。

You can propose some ideas about this project or any idea you want to share.
你們可以針對這個提案來提出建議或任何想分享的點子。

☕ **Any idea you would like to share?**
有任何想要分享的點子，都歡迎提出。

☕ **I would like to know if you guys have any ideas about this project.**
我想要知道你們對這個提案有沒有任何想法。

You could share the idea you have or the related experiences about the similar projects.
你可以分享你的想法，或是分享類似提案的經驗也可以。

I suggest we choose the best four cities and counties that are well known among the foreigners, and present the local cuisines and the related local tradition.
我建議，可以選擇台灣最具盛名的四個城市，來呈現在地美食及相關的在地傳統文化。

My suggestion is that we can choose the best four cities and counties that are well known among the foreigners, and present the local cuisines and the related local tradition.
我的建議是，可以選擇台灣最具盛名的四個城市，來呈現在地美食及相關的在地傳統文化。

In my opinion, we can present the local culture of the major cities in Taiwan with the local traditional foods.
我的意見是，我們可以用在地傳統食物來呈現台灣的主要城市的在地文化。

I suggest we use the local traditional foods to present the cultures and traditions of the major cities in Taiwan.
我建議，我們可以使用在地傳統食物來呈現台灣主要城市的文化及傳統。

Unit
08
參與國家爵士音樂暨美食節
Attending the National Jazz
and Cuisine Festival

8.1 情境對話──餐廳 CEO 和主廚間的討論
A discussion about the Preparation of
the National Jazz and Cuisine Festival

 Track 60

 CEO of The Big Mama, Mandy Lin Big Mama 營運長，Mandy Lin 小姐，簡稱 C。

 Chef of The Big Mama, Paolo, Big Mama 的主廚，Paolo 先生，簡稱 C。

The annual national jazz and cuisine festival is coming. Every year, the festival brings hundreds of thousands of people who love jazz music and many foreign cuisines. It's *The Big Mama*, an Italian handmade pizza factory, the first time to attend this festival and it wants to bring some fresh and new flavor pizzas made by their chef, Paolo Grosso. On Monday morning, Mandy Lin, the CEO of *The Big Mama*, is discussing the menu for the festival with chef Paolo.

C: Paolo, I have an idea. Based on my living experience in Italy, there are some differences between Taiwanese Italian food and the real Italian food. Most Taiwanese people do not have chances to taste the genuine Italian food. I think this is the best time to promote and introduce our restaurant. What do you think?

C: I agree with you about the concept you just mentioned. I think it's better to provide the customers with our genuine Italian cuisine made with a little change in the flavor so as to make a perfect match with the taste of the local people. We have to think about that because maybe there are customers like real Italian food, but others may not.

C: It does make sense! Ok, you are in charge of that part of the menu. Please give me the **draft** menu when you figure out what to make.

C: No problem!

Two days later...

C: Mandy, the menu for the festival is already done. Do you want to take a look?

C: That's ok, Paolo. I believe you will do everything well. I'll see you tomorrow in the festival.

Unit 08

中文翻譯

一年一度的爵士音樂季美食節即將到來。每年的爵士音樂暨美食節總是帶來成千上萬喜愛爵士音樂的及異國美食料理的人們來參加。**Big Mama** 義式手作披薩工房是第一次參與這個節日，他們想要帶來一些由主廚 **Paolo Grosso** 親自掌廚的新鮮及新口味的披薩。星期一早晨，**Big Mama** 義式手作披薩工房的營運長 **Mandy Lin**，正在與主廚 **Paolo** 討論要在音樂美食節推出的菜單。

C：Paolo，我有個點子。基於我在意大利生活的經驗，在台灣的義式料理與道地的義式料理還是有些差異。大部份的台灣人沒有嘗試過道地的義式料理。我想說，這是一個很好的機會，來推廣及介紹我們的餐廳。你覺得如何？

C：我同意妳剛剛說的概念。我想，最理想的方式是將道地的義式料理，做一點點小小的改變，讓在地的客人可以接受。我們必須去思考，或許有客人會喜愛道地的義式料理，但其他的人可能不喜歡。

C：這樣說很有道理。好，那菜單的部分就由你來負責了。若你已經想好菜色，再請讓我看一下菜單初稿。

C：沒問題。

兩天後……

C：Mandy，菜單已完成。你要看一下嗎？

C：不用了，Paolo。我想信你會把一切處理妥當的。明天爵士音樂節上見囉！

單字 Vocabulary

1. **bring** *v.* 帶
   例 Don't forget to bring your boarding pass before arriving at the airport.
   在抵達機場前，別忘了攜帶你的登機證。

2. **attend** *v.* 參加
   例 Would you like to attend Judy's birthday party this Friday night?
   週五晚上你想要參加 Judy 的生日聚會嗎？

3. **flavor** *n.* 口味
   例 There is just only one flavor of hotdog available in our store now.
   我們店裡現在只提供一種口味的熱狗。

4. **draft** *n.* 草稿
   例 My boss asked me to hand him the draft of proposal before the meeting.
   我的老闆要求我在會議前交出提案初稿給他。

Unit 08

8.2 情境對話——和家庭客的應答
Dialogue with Family Guests

 Track 61

Waiter 服務生，簡稱 W。

Guest 顧客，簡稱 G。

W: Today is the first day of the National Jazz and Cuisine Festival. There are some **genuine** Italian cuisines on sale now. We provide a fairly good price if they have our **chef**'s special. Once you order any main meal, we also provide a free appetizer for you.

G: What kind of main meals do you provide?

W: Here is the menu.

G: What do you recommend?

W: Sure, madam. Our chef's specials are Milano's dinner salad, smoked tuna with white wine and original hand-made pasta. We also provide pizzas with many kinds of flavor. Please turn to page six.

G: What kind of free appetizer can I get if I order the chef's special?

W: You can choose one of these two free appetizers, mozzarella with fresh tomato or French fries with cucumber.

G: Ok, then I would like to have one smoked tuna with white wine.

W: And your appetizer?

G: Mozzarella with fresh tomato, please.

W: Ok, madam. Would you like to have some coke?

G: No, thank you.

W: Ok. The total meal fee is $150. Here is your receipt and meal.

G: Thank you.

W: Thanks for your coming and we wish you a great night. Enjoy the beautiful jazz music.

Unit 08

中文翻譯

W：今天是爵士音樂季美食節的第一天。我們有一些道地義式美食正在折扣中喔。我們提供主廚特選餐，給品嚐爵士音樂的客人們一個非常超值的價格。一旦您購買任一主餐，我們就提供免費的前菜給您。

G：你們有提供哪些主餐？

W：這是菜單。

G：你可以介紹一下嗎？

W：當然可以的，女士。我們的主廚特選餐為米蘭主廚沙拉、煙燻鮪魚佐白酒及原味手做披薩。我們也有提供不同口味的披薩。請翻到第六頁。

G：若我點了主廚特選餐，你們提供哪些免費的前菜呢？

W：你可以選擇摩拉瑞拉起司佐新鮮蕃茄或是炸薯條佐黃瓜。

G：好，那麼我要點煙燻鮪鮪魚佐白酒。

W：那您的前菜要什麼呢？

G：摩拉瑞拉起司佐新鮮蕃茄。

W：好的，女士。您要來點可樂嗎？

G：不了，謝謝。

W：好的。總共餐費為 150 元。這是您的收據及餐點。

G：謝謝。

W：謝謝您的光臨，祝您有個美好的夜晚，有個美好的爵士音樂饗宴。

單字 Vocabulary

1. **genuine** *adj.* 道地的
   例 This restaurant provides genuine local traditional foods.
   這間餐廳提供道地的在底傳統美食。

2. **chef** *n.* 廚師
   例 Andy wants to be a chef when he grows up.
   Andy 長大後想當一名廚師。

Unit 08

8.3 情境對話——和團體客導遊的應答
Dialogue with Tour Guides

 Track 62

The salesman of the stand 展場攤位銷售員，簡稱 **S**。

Tour Guide, Jenny 導遊，*Jenny* 小姐，簡稱 **T**。

Tourist 遊客，簡稱 **T**。

T: Hello, I'm the Jenny, the tour guide of Big Apple Travel Agency. I'm here to pick up the jazz music tickets for 28 tourists I booked a week ago.

S: Hello, Jenny. How do you do? Are you ready for the show?

T: Yes, we are ready. Before we start, I would like to know how to use the food tickets **issued** by your restaurant.

S: Don't worry! I will make a brief introduction later.

T: Thanks.

S: No problem, it's my pleasure.

T: Ok, everyone, we are going in now. Please follow me.

Jenny leads the group into the exhibition, and the salesman is going to make a introduction about how to use the food tickets issued by the company.

S: Hello, welcome to the annual event here! I'm Joseph. I would like to tell you how to use the tickets. This ticket is not only the voucher of the music festival, but also the discount coupon for our delicious cuisine. You can come to our stand, use this coupon and taste the best ever Italian cuisine with the best jazz music. If you consume over $150, we will provide you an additional $100 coupon only available for our restaurant. If you need any further information, please come to our stand to get some food. We wish you have a good night here.

The music event starts, and there are more and more tourists coming to buy some food.

T: Hi, I would like to use this ticket to get some food.

S: Yes. What would you like to eat?

T: Can I have the menu?

S: Sure, here you are.

中文翻譯

T：哈囉，我是大蘋果旅行社大導遊 Jenny，我是來這取一週前訂的 28 位旅客的爵士音樂門票。

S：哈囉，Jenny，妳好嗎？你們準備好要入場囉？

T：是的，我們準備好了。在開始前，我想知道一下如何使用你們餐廳發行的餐飲票券。

S：別擔心，我待會兒會做個簡單介紹。

T：感謝。

S：不客氣，這是我的榮幸。

T：好的，各位，我們現在要進去囉。請跟著我。

Jenny 帶領團員進入會場，已及銷售人員正要進行介紹如何使用公司發行的餐飲票券……

S：哈囉，歡迎參加這個年度活動，我是活動負責人 Joseph。我想跟各位解說一下餐飲票的使用。這張票不只是音樂會票券，也是我們美食的折價券。你們可以來我們攤位上，用這張票券來品嚐最棒的義式料理，搭配最棒的爵士音樂。若您消費超過 $150，我們提供您額外的 $100 折價卷，給您來我們餐廳消費使用。若您有額外訊息，或是餓了想吃美食，都歡迎來我們攤位上。我們祝您今晚玩的愉快！

音樂盛宴開始進行，有許多旅客來找些食物了……

T：嗨，我想用這張票來拿些食物。

S：好的，您想吃些什麼呢？

T：我可以看一下菜單嗎？

S：當然，菜單給您。

單字 Vocabulary

1. issue *v.* 發行
   例 We only accept the official paper issued by us.
   我們僅接受我們發行的官方文件。

2. voucher *n.* 禮券
   例 You don't have to use the money but this voucher to purchase.
   你可不必使用現金購買，使用禮券即可。

Unit 08

8.4 換句話說 In Other Words

I think this is the best time to promote and introduce our restaurant.

我想說，這是一個很好的機會，來推廣及介紹我們的餐廳。

This is a good chance for us to promote the foods and beverages in our restaurant.

這是一個很好的機會來推廣我們餐廳的餐點及飲品。

We have an opportunity to promote our fantastic foods to the potential customers.

我們有個機會來好好推廣我們超棒的美食給潛在的顧客。

We can introduce our restaurant by this chance and let our potential customers know the bestselling cuisines.

我們可以藉由這次機會來介紹我們餐廳，以及給客人知道我們銷售最好的美食有哪些。

Most Taiwanese people do not have the chances to taste the genuine Italian food.

大部份的台灣人沒有嘗試過道地的義式料理。

There are few genuine Italian food providers her in Taiwan.

在台灣很少有真正道地的義式餐點提供者。

It's hard to find a restaurant that provides real Italian food in Taiwan.

在台灣很難找到提供道地義式料理的餐廳。

☕ **Only a few Italian restaurants provide the genuine cuisine in Taiwan**.

在台灣，只有少數幾間義式餐廳提供道地的料理。

I think it's better to provide the customers with our genuine Italian cuisine made with a little change in the flavor so as to make a perfect match with the taste of the local people.

我想，最理想的方式是將道地的義式料理，做一點點小小的改變，讓在地的客人可以接受。

☕ **For the local Taiwanese consumers, we can make some changes in the flavor of Italian food**.

為了讓在地台灣消費者接受道地義式料理，我們可以做一些小改變。

☕ **We have to make some changes in flavors to meet Taiwanese customers' requirements**.

我們必須在口味上做些改變來滿足在地台灣客人的需求。

☕ **It's good to modifiy the menu by making some changes in flaovrs to meet the Taiwanese customers' requirements**.

為滿足台灣客人的需求，加入一些新口味的方式來修改菜單是很好的。

職場補給站 Must-Know Tips

有時候我們難免會有聽不懂外籍旅客或客人的詢問（inquiry），千萬別緊張，以下教你幾招如何請對方在敘述一次的用語。

☆ Would you speak slowly, please?

請您說慢一點好嗎？

☆ I beg your pardon. = Pardon me? = Pardon?

對不起，您剛才說什麼？

☆ I didn't hear you clearly.

我沒聽清楚您說的。

☆ Could you please express by a simple word?

您可以用簡單一點的方式說嗎？

☆ Would you please repeat it again?

您可以在重複一次嗎？

若真的沒有辦法處理外籍旅客或客人的問題時，只好尋找救兵了。這時候可以請外籍旅客或客人稍等，你將另請他人提供協助：

☆ Please wait a second; I'll call another waiter / receptionist to give you assistance.

請稍等，我將請另外一名服務生／櫃檯人員來提供您協助。

重要句型整理 Useful Sentences

① **Business set is available for lunch and dinner.**
商務餐有提供午餐及晚餐。

② **Would you like some appetizers?**
請問你需要來點開胃菜嗎？

③ **When would you like to pick up your meal?**
請問您什麼時候要來取餐呢？

④ **May I get your name, phone number and the address to deliver your order?**
請提供您的名字、電話號碼及地址，以方便我們替您送餐？

⑤ **Is smoking permitted here?**
這裡可以吸菸嗎？

⑥ **May I briefly introduce our service for you?**
請問我可以為您簡單介紹一下餐廳服務嗎？

⑦ **It's great to hear from you again.**
很開心再次聽到您的來電。

⑧ **Then your reservation is conformed.**
已確認您的訂位了。

⑨ **How would you like to make your payment?**
您要怎麼支付呢？

⑩ **Anything else we can do for you?**
請問還有別的需要嗎？

Leader 044

Easy & Basic 餐飲口說英語（附 MP3）

作　　　者	林書平
發 行 人	周瑞德
執行總監	齊心瑀
企劃編輯	饒美君
校　　　對	編輯部
封面構成	高鍾琪

內頁構成	華漢電腦排版有限公司
印　　　製	大亞彩色印刷製版股份有限公司
初　　　版	2016 年 05 月
定　　　價	新台幣 380 元
出　　　版	力得文化
電　　　話	(02) 2351-2007
傳　　　真	(02) 2351-0887
地　　　址	100 台北市中正區福州街 1 號 10 樓之 2
E - m a i l	best.books.service@gmail.com
網　　　址	www.bestbookstw.com

港澳地區總經銷	泛華發行代理有限公司
地　　　址	香港新界將軍澳工業邨駿昌街 7 號 2 樓
電　　　話	(852) 2798-2323
傳　　　真	(852) 2796-5471

國家圖書館出版品預行編目資料

Easy & Basic 餐飲口說英語 / 林書平著. -- 初版.

-- 臺北市：力得文化, 2016.05

　面；　　公分. -- (Leader ; 44)

ISBN 978-986-92856-3-6 (平裝附光碟片)

1.英語　2.餐飲業　3.會話

805.188　　　　　　　　　　105005954